John Jasper Wyeth

Leaves from a Diary written while serving in Co. E, 44 Mass.

Dep't of No. Carolina, from September 1862 to June 1863

John Jasper Wyeth

Leaves from a Diary written while serving in Co. E, 44 Mass.
Dep't of No. Carolina, from September 1862 to June 1863

ISBN/EAN: 9783337018306

Printed in Europe, USA, Canada, Australia, Japan

Cover: Foto ©Andreas Hilbeck / pixelio.de

More available books at **www.hansebooks.com**

LEAVES FROM A DIARY

WRITTEN WHILE SERVING IN

CO. E
DEP'T OF 44 NO.CAROLINA
MASS.

FROM SEPTEMBER, 1862, TO JUNE, 1863.

BOSTON :
L. F. LAWRENCE & CO., 169 DEVONSHIRE ST.
1878.

PREFACE.

Boston, April, 1878.

Comrades of " E."

If you find this little history does not treat of our experiences, in as full a manner as you might expect, please remember that at the time it was written, I had little thought of ever arranging it for publication.

Though the desire to write was strong, the flesh was very weak, many times, especially after a twenty-four hour guard, with a subsequent four to five hours' police duty ; or while on a tramp through those sandy roads of North Carolina.

I am afraid, the disinclination of a boy at 19 to apply his ideas to a work of this kind, when he was tired and hungry, mastered many of the Company, who now wish they had carried a memorandum book, and used it.

Our service, as you are aware, was tame beside that of some others. But was that our fault ? I think it is not too much to say that we never refused to do our duty, and if we had no opportunity it was no fault, but perhaps our misfortune, that we were not assigned to a department where we might have been used up in a month or two.

We enlisted in those " Dark days of '62," at the call of President Lincoln, for nine months' troops. No promises were held out to us that we would not be put to as severe tests of courage, or have a chance to achieve as great deeds of heroism, as any who had preceded us. I doubt if there was one who asked or thought of where he was going, as he signed the roll at Mercantile Hall.

We soon learned, to our sorrow, that a bullet could maim and kill, as well at Rawle's Mills, as at Antietam, as well in a short, as a long campaign.

Afterwards, as our Roster shows, many returned to the service, who did honor, not only to themselves, but to the school from which they graduated.

JOHN J. WYETH,

Late of Co. E, 44th Mass. Vols.

THIS LITTLE VOLUME IS DEDICATED

TO OUR CAPTAIN;

WHO, BY HIS CONSTANT CARE

AND WATCH OVER US,

WON OUR RESPECT FOR ALL TIME.

THE ORGANIZATION.

On the evening of August 7th, 1862, the 4th Battalion Infantry (New England Guard) held a meeting at their Armory, Boylston Hall, Boston, Major Francis L. Lee presiding. It was resolved unanimously to respond to the order of Gen. Davis, and to accept the offer of Gov. Andrew for the battalion to recruit to a regiment. At the call for members to sign the new roll, there was a general rush, each being anxious to get his name on the list first ; between two and three hundred men enlisted. On the same day the battalion paraded the city, with Flagg's band. This battalion was the nucleus of our regiment, our company being raised by Mr. Spencer W. Richardson, under the auspices of the Mercantile Library Association, of Boston (of which organization he was a prominent member), with the assistance of Messrs. James S. Newell and James S. Cumston. Our head-quarters being in the large hall of the Association on Summer Street.

AUGUST 11.—Mr. Richardson reported at a meeting held by the Association, that he had obtained fifty-six excellent recruits since Thursday, all of them as good men as are employed in the principal business streets of the city. Six more joined at this meeting. A resolution was adopted to make all recruits of this company members of the Association. Speeches were made by Hon. A. H. Rice, Ex-Gov. Washburne, Lt. W. E. Richardson, of the 33d M. V., and others.

AUGUST 14.—The Mercantile Hall Company was reported as having fifteen more men than the number required. The recruits were all young and able-bodied, great care being taken to enlist such men only, as it was thought, would pass the surgical examination.

AUGUST 20.—Our company held a meeting yesterday, and chose the following as officers : Captain, Spencer W. Richardson ; First Lieutenant, James S. Newell; Second Lieutenant, James S. Cumston.

AT READVILLE.

AUGUST 29.—A busy day for Co. E ; we have been ordered to camp. Each man was told to carry rations enough for two meals. We formed company for the first time, out of doors, on the Boylston Street Mall ; marched to the Boston and Providence Depot, and after hand-shaking with our friends, went aboard the cars, arriving at Readville, ten miles out, at four o'clock; and here the troubles and tribulations of many a fine young man began. We found that either the regiment had come too soon or the carpenters had been lazy, for only three of the ten barracks were roofed, and some were not even boarded in, so while the carpenters went at work outside, we went at it inside, putting up and fixing the bunks.

About sunset, we saw a load of straw on the way to our barracks ; at first we supposed it was for bedding for horses, but we were green. It was to take the place of hair mattresses. Could it be! that Uncle Samuel proposed that we should sleep in the straw ? (I remember when a youngster, of going to Brighton, to see the soldiers just home from the Mexican war, they had straw in their tents to sleep on. I little thought then, that I should be jumping upon the wheels of a wagon, tugging for straw enough for a bed, but such was the fact,) straw was used, but for a very little while by most of us.

After our first supper (and a gay picnic one it was) in this wilderness, we sang songs, told stories, formed new, and found old acquaintances, until after eight o'clock. Then for the first time in camp, we heard " Fall in Co. E ;" the roll was called, and it was found that of the one hundred and twenty-five names ninty-nine had reported. Our captain made a little speech, to which of course we did not reply ; and then for bed. We had (that is the quiet ones) made up our minds for a good night's rest, so as to be all right for the arduous duties of the morrow. There were some however, who thought noise and confusion the first law of a soldier. It was late, and not until after several visits from the officers that the boys decided to quiet down.

August 30.—Our first morning in camp. We were rudely awakened and dragged from our bunks at six o'clock, very few being used to such early hours, except perhaps on 4th of July, and were expected to be on the parade ground before our eyes were fairly open.

My advice is if you ever enlist again, start with buckle or congress boots, or none at all, don't wear laced ones. Why ? Thereby hangs a tale. One man who wore laced boots was late, consequently had to fall in at the foot of the column. In a minute or two, around came the adjutant and some other officer, who wanted a man for guard. The man who was late at roll-call, was detailed of course. He went without a word ; was posted on the edge of a pond ; his orders being—" Keep this water from being defiled, allow no privates to bathe here, let only the officers bathe *and the cooks draw water to cook with.*" The orders were fulfilled, but the poor guard was forgotten, and paced up and *mostly down* (as it was a pleasant grassy sward,) till eleven o'clock. That was his first experience of guard duty, and he always owed a grudge to the sergeant of that guard and his laced boots.

Meanwhile, the company, left standing in the street, with their towels, combs, &c., proceeded to the water, where the pride of many a family got down on his knees, and went through the farce of a toilet, and then back to breakfast.

To-day we have been busy cleaning up and getting ready for our friends from home. It has been as novel a day as last night was new, it is a great change, but we will conquer this, and probably worse.

Our friends began to arrive about three o'clock, and by supper-time the barracks were well filled, many remaining to supper ; so shawls and blankets were spread upon the ground, and we gave them a sample of our food. The coffee was good but so hot, and having no saucer with which to cool the beverage, we had to leave it till the last course. Our plates were plated with tin, but very shallow, and as bean soup was our principal course we had some little trouble in engineering it from the cook's quarters to our tables. We must not forget the bread, it was made by the State, and by the looks, had been owned by the State since the Mexican war. We had never seen the like, and begged to be excused from enduring much of it at a time. (We afterwards found no occasion to grumble at our food, for as you may remember, we were looked after *well during our whole service.* We had as good rations as any one could wish, but here, within ten miles of home, we felt that this was *rough on the boys.*)

For a week, little was done but feed and drill us, to toughen us for the dim future, and the furloughs were granted very freely. We were soon astonished to find that we had for a surgeon, a man who meant business. Among other things, he thought government clothes were all that we needed, so *spring and fall overcoats* and fancy dry goods had to be bundled up and sent home. All our good things were cleaned out, everything was contraband excepting what the government allowed. We had always thought it a free country, but this broke in on our individual ideas of personal freedom, and we began to think we were fast losing all trace of civil rights, and becoming soldiers pure and simple. Nothing could be brought into camp by our friends unless we could eat it before the next morning : but goodies would come, and as we had to eat them, of course we were sick.

SEPTEMBER 5.—We have had several dress parades, in which we made a creditable appearance, considering the fact that no arms had been issued. On presenting the battalion to the commanding officer instead of the command " Present Arms," as we had none to present, the order was " Salute," which we executed as only recruits can.

We have had rumors, not of war, but Muster in ; in the meantime the boys are generally up to something or other, to relieve the monotony of " Left," " Left," " Left," from day to day. Some companies have attached flag-staffs to the fronts of the barracks, and our captain not wishing to be behind any others, ordered a detail to proceed to some man's wood-lot and cut a suitable stick." We started with hatchets, tramping towards the Blue Hills, and finally secured a fine tall tree, which we cut, trimmed, and shouldered to camp, and putting it in position found it to be tallest in the line.

Geo. Russell kindly furnished us with a large flag and then " E " was high line. There is much emulation among the companies to be the one to lower the flag first, at sunset ; Russell attached about two pounds of lead to the hallyards, close to the flag, thoroughly greased the pulley, and then all it needed was one strong pull, and a pull altogether, and down comes the flag ; the quickest of any although our pole is much the tallest.

SEPTEMBER 10.—Our barracks look finely now, and we are getting much more accustomed to soldiers' life. We have had continuous drilling, our officers taking turns drilling us, but here is where the difference comes in between officers and men; they take turns tramping us up and down that old field, while we take turns every time. It is hardly six of one and half-dozen of the other.

SEPTEMBER 12.—One of the days to be remembered, having had a deeper experience of life than ever before. Early in the day orders came to put on our best rig, and get ready to be sworn in, as a mustering officer was coming to camp to perform that (to Uncle Sam) very important duty. Our company was drawn up facing the head-quarters for a long time. The boys being in a fever of excitement as to how the operation would work, whether it would hurt much, or whether the home-folks would know us ever afterward. It turned out about as *easy* as the measles; some itching for a while, but soon over. The officer, Captain N. B. McLaughlin, of the Regular Army, walked up and down each rank as we stood in open order; looking at each man; picking out one or two and punching them a little, probably to scare them as much as possible; intending to pass them all. Then, coming in front of us while our hats were off and right hands raised, repeated the oath of service, and we were finally soldiers of the Volunteer Army. We felt that we were taller men by at least ten inches, and it is possible if Sergeant Thayer had measured the company then and there it would have been one of the tallest. But it was still "Left," "Left," "Left," again, and we soon found our level.

We are a social party; hardly a day but brings crowds from the city. Our company has its share. One afternoon quite a party of young ladies were with us trying to keep up our spirits. They were to stay awhile in the evening, going home by the late train, so we thought we would get up a little dance, but half-past eight o'clock came all to quickly, they had to go; and then the question arose how were we to see them to the cars. Try our best we could only spare one man. That lucky individual, whoever he was, will remember the incident. As this was probably the young ladies' last visit before our start for the South, we demanded and received our last good-bye kisses, but when they saw the same boys falling in the second time, and some of them strangers, they scattered like a drove of sheep over the fences and far away to the station. I think that was the last effort the company made (as an orgaization) to kiss them *all* a good-bye.

SEPTEMBER 14.—Our guns are on the field somewhere, they are Enfield rifles, and report says they are good ones; they have been distributed to the guard, but it is said owing to the lack of racks in our barracks it will be several days before we get them. It is reported that our arms are a lot captured from a blockade runner, and intended for the rebels. We don't care much where they come from or for whom they were intended, if they are made so they won't kill at both ends.

SEPTEMBER 16.—To-day, for a change, we had permission to drill outside the lines, and Orderly White, at the earnest solicitation of some of us, took the company to Dedham on a double quick, Dedham is about four miles from camp, and after the first hill, close to the old house where we used to run guard and get pies and

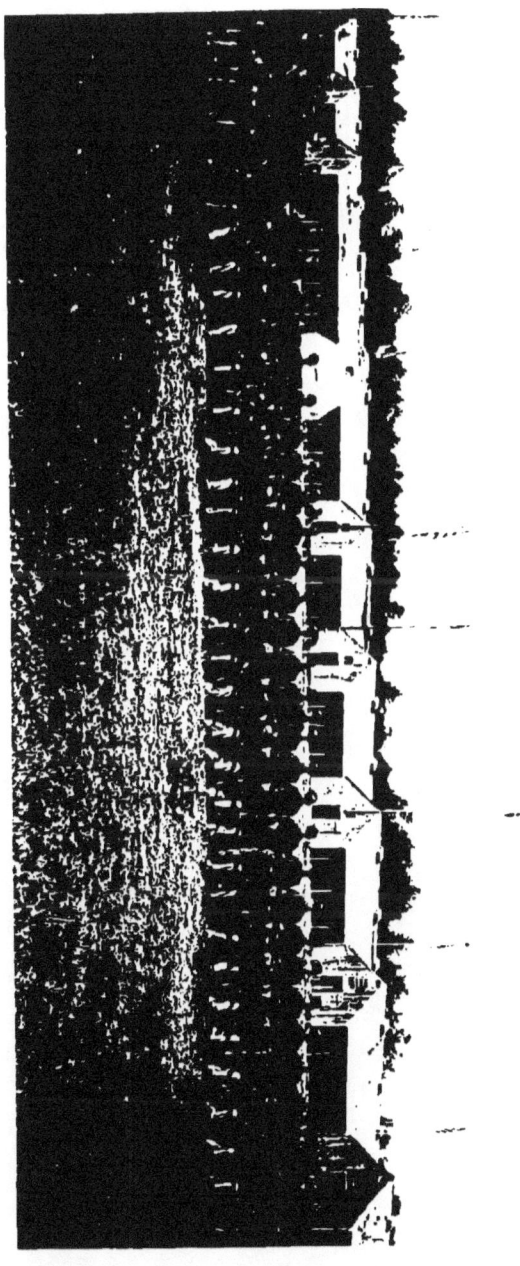

READVILLE, SEPT., 1862.

cakes, it is a very level and easy run; we never stopped the steady jog till we reached the Phœnix House. Only one man fell out; but nothing but pride kept many of us in the line. It was the first attempt at such work, and came like drawing teeth. The orderly was level-headed enough not to let us drink anything for sometime, but after we had rested about fifteen minutes and cooled off, he obtained some lemonade, which was excellent.

We then formed line and started back to camp, returning by a different road, arriving there about four o'clock P.M., and then the orderly thought of the battalion drill, ordered at half-past three. As we looked down on the camp from the old railroad track, back of the barracks, we could see the regiment in line, and the grounds crowded with our friends. We had no conversation with the colonel on this subject, but soon found out he was mad, for we were put in the street next our barracks, and guards placed at each end, not even being allowed to go into the barrack to wash up, and our friends were denied us. We stood there in disgrace till dress parade. We were very much *afraid* the whole company would be *discharged the service*. There were some rumors of breaking the orderly, but they did not do so. We did not run away much after that.

SEPTEMBER 20.—We have had another pleasure curtailed. It has been the practice for the boys to go to the pond by the railroad, and dive off the bank which slopes here very abruptly, enjoying the swimming very much, but some of the soldiers must be very sensitive (as no one else lives within shooting distance of the pond), and orders have come from head-quarters to stop all bathing. This order must have come from higher authority than our regiment, and we are obliged to go up the track a half mile or so, where we had considerable fun, one day in particular; the place was the scene of much sport. While a squad under Corporal Cartwright were bathing, the question arose, whether we could throw any one across the creek. Cartwright volunteered to be the subject, and having partly dressed, was thrown head first; of course he did no go half way across, and had the pleasure of going to camp wet.

Some of the members of the Mercantile Library Association, friends of Capt. Richardson, have presented him with a fine sword, sash, &c.

The guard have mysteriously lost some of their rifles, we cannot imagine where, but suppose the officers know If any of " E " have suffered, they do not tell any " tales out of school."

SEPTEMBER 24.—Our rifles have been delivered, and to-day we were in line two hours or more on the main street of the camp, ready to receive, with military honors, Col. Stevenson, of the 24th Regiment, but he did not come. The boys say he purposely delayed his visit, so as to avoid that ceremony. Many of our company drilled under him in the battalion and liked him very much.

We are mad with the Sutler. We think he charges too much for things which our friends would gladly bring us, so, many will not trade with him, and many things are still smuggled through the lines. If we could only get up our spunk to clean him out. Some one with malicious intent and forethought, did break into his domicile and start things, but were frightened, or, probably belonging to some other regiment, did not know how our account stood.

SEPTEMBER 27. — On Thursday last, we performed our first public duty, after drilling in the loadings and firings, in which we excelled, after firing "higher" several times. Six companies, of which "E" was one, under command of Lieut.-Col. Cabot, started for Jamaica Plain, by the Providence Railroad, to attend the funeral of Lieut.-Col. Dwight, of the 2nd Mass Vols., who died of wounds on the 13th of September. We performed escort duty to the grave where we fired three very creditable volleys, considering our practice. When we arrived at camp that afternoon "E" was decidedly cross, and we well remember the sight, as we marched to our quarters, we could not imagine what could be the matter, great piles of what looked to us like rubbish in front and rear of the barracks, proved to be our all. In fact every blessed thing but our government clothes and blankets were to go by the board. All the extra comforts, the fancy signs on our bunks. even Miller lost his chicken, and accused one of the innocents, who was left at the camp to help to clean up, with taking it. The unfortunate man will be known always as Chicken Hayes among the few evil-minded men of the company, who really think Hayes fraudulently reached for that chicken. We were a sorry set, but wondered if the despoliation was as thorough in the officers' tents. We never found out, for we visited there very seldom, and were there only upon business of more importance. It was called a sanitary improvement to rob us of all these little things. The boys did not cater for such improvements at all.

OCTOBER 2.—We have had two practice-marches lately, one a long one, in Milton Hill direction, where we found plenty of dust, but were assured we were making muscle ; and the last to Dedham Village, were we were very pleasantly received by the people, especially the ladies. Those of us who could, cleared out and introduced ourselves (temporarily) among the first families, and were feasted right royally. We had hardly arrived at camp again from this expedition, the object of which we accomplished, when we were startled with rumors that our regiment was ordered off. Some said to the Potomac, some to New Orleans, and others to North Carolina. The general idea seems to be that no one knows much about it, and one young lady was heard to say, "Well, I am going to New York Tuesday, to be gone three months, and I don't believe, but that the boys will be in Readville when I come back ; any way, I won't say good-bye for good." If we go to New Berne, it is expected and hoped by the 4th Battalion men that they will be brigaded with Col. Stevenson, giving him a star. There has been quite a discussion about our knapsacks. The boys don't want the army style, but if the other companies have it, we probably will have to put up with it, many would care nothing for any kind, and probably whichever we have, some will throw them away. There is talk that all the companies will have "Shorts."

Wm. Cumston, Esq., father of our second lieutenant, has presented the boys with five hundred dollars, as a fund to use in case of sickness. to buy fresh food with. It is a noble present, and the boys fully appreciate it.

OCTOBER 17. — We have had another march, this time about ten miles, through Dedham and towards Boston ; the nearest we came to the city was West Roxbury. Probably we will not see much more of Boston, for the rumors are getting thicker and more substantial; but on this march, the boys who went, saw enough to make them wish to keep on to the city.

Our company is under great obligations to the following Boston gentlemen for the sum of three hundred dollars, with which to buy the patent knapsack:— J. M. Beebe & Co., F. Skinner & Co., Alex. Beal, C. W. Cartwright, W. P. Sargent, Read, Gardner & Co., Wilkinson, Stetson & Co., Horatio Harris, J. R. Tibbets, E. & F. King & Co., G. Rogers, and J. C. Converse & Co.; and it is understood measures are being taken to furnish the other companies, so we will be equipped alike. The only trouble being can they be finished in time. This week which looks like the last one to be passed here, has been dismal enough, it has rained a good part of the time, and to crown all, *we can't smoke in the barracks.* Corporals or no corporals, it is hard work to keep us down. We had a fair time, and many a smoke under cover.

Some one has seen a box of one of the staff officers, marked New Berne, so unless it was a blind, that is our destination, the boys don't care much where, but only to get started. The last few days have finished the business ; it is muddy, damp, and growing colder gradually, and we want to get away. Our last fur-loughs are gone, and the sooner we go the better.

OCTOBER 20.—We had orders to start Wednesday morning for Boston, to embark on a transport for New Berne, North Carolina. A very few men were let off once more, but only for a few hours. Worse than none at all, but eagerly sought for by all. Notwithstanding the strict orders relative to extras in our barracks all had many things to send home, and the express companies had plenty to do till the very last. Tuesday night came finally, and after about eight weeks' camp life, which had been novel to most of us, we were to start early in the morning for something new to the whole. We made a late evening, having a gay and noisy time, excepting a few of us, who were on guard; we had the excitement without the means of allaying or counteracting it, but paced our beats thinking of all the trouble and tribulation which might be in store for us.

OCTOBER 22.—We broke camp bright and early, about six o'clock, had our last bath at the pond, and breakfast at the old barracks, which had been our home so long, and then commenced the packing of our knapsacks and haversacks, till about eight o'clock, when we fell in with the rest of the regiment, and about nine o'clock marched to the station. After a fine salute from the 45th, who were drawn up on the hill at the right of the railroad track, we started for Boston. We marched to the Common, where we found our friends once more. We stayed here about an hour, talking the last talk for many a long week, then fell into line, and escorted by the New England Guard Reserve and other organizations, we took our way up Beacon Street, down Tremont, Court, State, and Commercial, to Battery Wharf to the steamer "Merrimac." Here we had a rest, and we needed it, our knapsacks were full, and the tramp was hard on us. Many of our friends smuggled themselves through the line at the head of the Wharf, and we held our last reception once more. Our guns were taken from us here, and finally we were packed away too, in the lower hold ; no light, and about the same quantity of air. We left the Wharf about six o'clock, the cheers of our friends following us far out into the stream.

Our reception while passing through the city was a fine one, the streets were crowded, especially State Street, and we were cheered from one end of it to the other. We leave plenty of friends, as the following clipped from the *Transcript* will show :

DEPARTURE OF MASS. REGIMENTS FOR NEW BERNE.

The city has been thronged by strangers to-day to witness the arrival in the city of the three Mass. Regiments, and their embarkation on board the steamers which are to convey them to New Berne.

The " Forty Fourth," which has been encamped at Readville, *absorbed the chief interest of the citizens of Boston.* This regiment is the child of the New England Guard, and from its appearance, will worthily maintain its hereditary honor. It is the second regiment recruited by prominent members of the Guards, and is largely composed of young men who will be sadly missed here.

The hold the Forty-fourth has upon the sympathies and affections of our community has been shown to-day by the large turn-out to greet the boys as they went through the city.

The scene in the vicinity of Boylston Street was of quite an exhilarating character. The streets were filled with people, and windows and balconies contained large numbers of the fair sex, who waved their heart-welcome for the soldiers as they marched along.

Company H, Capt. Smith, had the right, and Company A, Capt. J. M. Richardson, the left.

Crowds thronged the avenues through which the troops passed, and loudly applauded them. The Forty-fourth marched almost with the steady tread of veterans, and by their precision of movement deserved the applause so liberally bestowed. The Roster is as follows:

Colonel	Francis L. Lee.
Lieut.-Colonel	Edward C. Cabot.
Major	Chas. W. Dabney, Jr.
Adjutant	Wallace Hinckley.
Quarter-Master	Francis Bush, Jr.
Surgeon	Robert Ware.
Assistant Surgeon	Theodore W. Fisher.
Chaplain	Edmund H. Hall.
Sergt-Major	Wm. H. Bird.
Quarter-Master-Sergt.	Fred. S. Gifford.
Commissary Sergt.	Charles D. Woodberry.
Hospital Steward	Wm. C. Brigham.
Principal Musician	Geo. L. Babcock.

COMPANY A.
Captain—James M. Richardson.
1st Lt.—Jared Coffin.
2nd Lt.—Charles G. Kendall.

COMPANY B.
Captain—John M. Griswold.
1st Lt.—John A. Kendrick, Jr.
2nd Lt.—Charles C. Soule.

COMPANY C.
Captain—Jacob H. Lombard.
1st Lt.—George B. Lombard.
2nd Lt.—James W. Briggs.

COMPANY D.
Captain—Henry D. Sullivan.
1st Lt.—James H. Blake, Jr.
2nd Lt.—Asa H. Stebbins.

COMPANY E.
Captain—Spencer W. Richardson.
1st Lt.—James S. Newell.
2nd Lt.—James S. Cumston.

COMPANY F.
Captain—Charles Storrow.
1st Lt.—Alfred S. Hartwell.
2nd Lt.—John E. Taylor.

COMPANY G.
Captain—Charles Hunt.
1st Lt.—James C. White.
2nd Lt.—Frederick Odiorne.

COMPANY H.
Captain—William V. Smith.
1st Lt.—Edward C. Johnson.
2nd Lt.—Albert R. Howe.

COMPANY I.
Captain—Joseph R. Kendall.
1st Lt.—William D. Hooper.
2nd Lt.—Benjamin F. Field, Jr.

COMPANY K.
Captain—Frank W. Reynolds.
2nd Lt.—Richard H. Weld.
2nd Lt.—Fred. P. Brown.

OCTOBER 23.—Most of us, when we turned in last night, thought by the time we went on deck this morning, we would be far from land. We were mistaken. The steamer had only gone as far as the Roads, where she anchored.

About five o'clock this morning we made the final start for the war, unless Davy Jones shall have a mind to claim us. There are a few boats; but then there are, besides our regiment, about 500 of the 3d Mass. Vols., Col. Richmond, making about 1500 men in addition to the ship's crew. Sea voyages, as we are taking this one, are anything but pleasant. We know nothing of what is going on, and are very much crowded, in what would be good quarters for half the number. But the boys cannot appreciate this any more than they can to see the beef, which we are to eat, dragged across the deck, which, in the neighborhood of the horse stalls, is not very clean.

OCTOBER 24.—Last night, about nine o'clock, we passed through Vineyard Sound, and saw the last of Old Massachusetts, of which we shall probably see nothing for nearly a year. There will be very little excitement now, for two or three days, excepting we speak other vessels, so the boys are going to improve the time in sleeping and eating. To-day, one of our company, Edward Richardson, was taken sick and carried to the hospital. He is the first to succumb, owing in a great measure, we think, to the foul air of our quarters. This afternoon we saw the "Alabama" (or thought we did), on our quarter, and of course would have been sold out cheap, as our boat was not armed, and our consort was nowhere to be seen.

OCTOBER 25.—We turned in last night in a commotion, for if the "Alabama" should overhaul us what should we do? We could not defend ourselves, nor could we swim ashore. We soon saw, by the way the officers of our boat allowed the other to overhaul us, that they were not afraid. It turned out to be our old friend the "Mississippi," with the 5th Mass., the balance of the 3d, and a few of ours, who had been left behind. We found afterwards that the men on the other steamer were as frightened as we were, thinking us the "Alabama." Why were the officers so reticent? What needless anxiety they could have saved by promulgating what they knew.

Many had become so tired of sleeping below that they tried the deck and boats, but were always driven down, not at the point of the bayonet, but with a handspike. Two of us arranged a novel sleeping place, and proposed to try it ; we got into the chains and tied ourselves to the shrouds, where we could lie and watch the phosphorus below, and wonder if a sudden lurch would shake us off into the drink ; but were reserved for another though similar fate, for towards morning we were awakened by a disagreeably damp sensation, and found ourselves drenched with the rain, so we hauled down our colors and crawled below to shake out the balance of the night.

ARRIVAL AT NEW BERNE.

OCTOBER 26.—About nine this morning we saw our first of Rebeldom, and after taking a pilot, and passing several ugly-looking rips and bars, leaving Fort Macon on our left, we disembarked from the steamer to the wharf, which had a railroad depot on the farther end of it. The place is called Morehead City. But if this is a city, what can the towns and villages be? We stayed in this shed or depot awhile, and were then ordered on the train of open cars. Here we waited for two mortally long hours in a pelting rain, water on each side of us, water over us, and gradually, but persistently, water all through our clothes, and not a drop of *anything* inside of us.

Notwithstanding the rain storm was severe, we had considerable to interest us after we started, which was between two and three o'clock. There had been fighting along the line of road a year previous, and every few miles we passed picket-posts, occupied by Mass. regiments. We cheered them and they responded. Once, where we stopped to wood-up, we saw a settlement of negroes, and some of the boys bought or hooked their first sweet potatoes here. Others of us contented ourselves with trying to keep our pipes lighted, our tobacco dry, and the cinders out of our eyes. Most all of us came to the conclusion that North Carolina was a tough place, barren and desolate, and hardly worth the cost of fighting for it.

We arrived at New Berne about six o'clock, wet through, hungry, tired, and ready for our feather beds, but found our hotel for that night was not supplied with any such articles of furniture.

Our company, with some others, was quartered in a big barn of a building built of green boards, which had shrunk both side and end ways, and for beds we had the floor, with a few bundles of hay scattered around. We could not expect much of a supper, but we managed some way, and then turned in, wet as we were. Soon after, we were called up and informed that coffee and beef, with compliments, from the Mass. 24th Reg't, were awaiting. We accepted, with thanks, and made quite a supper. Then we turned in again,—some on bundles of hay, others on the floor. Those on the hay had a hard time of it, as the bundles were shorter than we were, and we had a tendency also to roll off. So after several ineffectual attempts, many gave it up and started from the building to find better quarters. Finally, we found some wood, made a rousing fire in an old sugar boiler, and stood around it in the rain, trying to keep warm, if not dry.

OCTOBER 27.—We worried through the dismal, wet night, and morning found us hungry again, so we scattered. Our breakfasts were picked up here and there, but there was such a novelty about everything that nothing would do but to have a walk about town. New Berne is a very fair sample of a Southern town, splendidly laid out in regard to the streets and trees, but the buildings have a deserted, forlorn look, probably from want of paint and care. We had a good time for a while, but soon found the provost guard obnoxious They asked too many questions, and finally ordered us out of the town altogether. We went back to quarters, and found the company gone; only a sergeant left, to pick up stragglers. We straggled with him towards camp, appreciating the thoughtfulness of the captain in leaving some one to show us where the head-quarters were.

OCTOBER 28.—We have been hard at work yesterday and to-day fixing up our camp, which is located about a quarter of a mile from town on the old race-course. There are troops stationed in our neighborhood in every direction. Quite a village ; but our time so far has been too much employed at home to do much visiting. We are in tents, nineteen men to a tent. We have been banking and boarding up, to prepare for bad weather, although our barracks are nearly done, and we hope to get into them soon. We are very much crowded in our tent, but have plenty of fresh air, of which we have had very little for a week, and are correspondingly thankful. Rumors are beginning to come ; we have them to-night that we are going to into the Wilderness immediately. Our tent is comparatively vacant, as this afternoon five were taken out for night guard on a supply train.

OCTOBER 29.—Those of us who are on guard to-day are having a " soft time." We have our orders to start at three to-morrow morning. The boys are busy packing, receiving cartridges, &c.; the cooks are hard at work in their department, and the surgeon is hunting for men to guard camp. We were afraid the guard were to be left, but the captain says he won't forget us. The knapsacks are to be stored in the officers' tents, and we are ordered to get all the sleep we can from now till four to-morrow, perhaps the last nap under cover for weeks.

OUR FIRST MARCH.

OCTOBER 30.—This morning, at four o'clock, we thought the Old Nick was to pay, but soon found it was only the long roll. It would have sounded better if a little later, but we got up just the same, formed in line, marched across the city, and embarked aboard the steamer " Geo. Collins." The old saying about large bodies and their slowness, applied here ; we might have slept two hours longer, for it was nine o'clock before we started. The vessel had evidently just returned from a voyage with cattle on board, so all who could, remained on deck. We were well paid, for the scenery for fifteen miles was fine ; after that the banks of the river were swampy and dismal. We saw a portion of the old fighting ground of the last year when Mass. troops fought to obtain possession of New Berne.

We passed into the sound about three o'clock, and at dark had not entered the Pamlico river, so supper and bunks were in order. The supper was -fair, but " distance lent enchantment to the " smell of the bunks.

OCTOBER 31.—At daybreak we were well into the river, and at noon reached Little Washington. At home, this would be a small, and decidedly second-class town, here it is a city. It is well located on the banks of the river, and with energy might be made quite a place. We marched to the easterly end of the town to a large open field, and pitched camp. Not even tents this time. But we found a lot of box boards, and soon had comfortable bunks. Many of them like coffins,

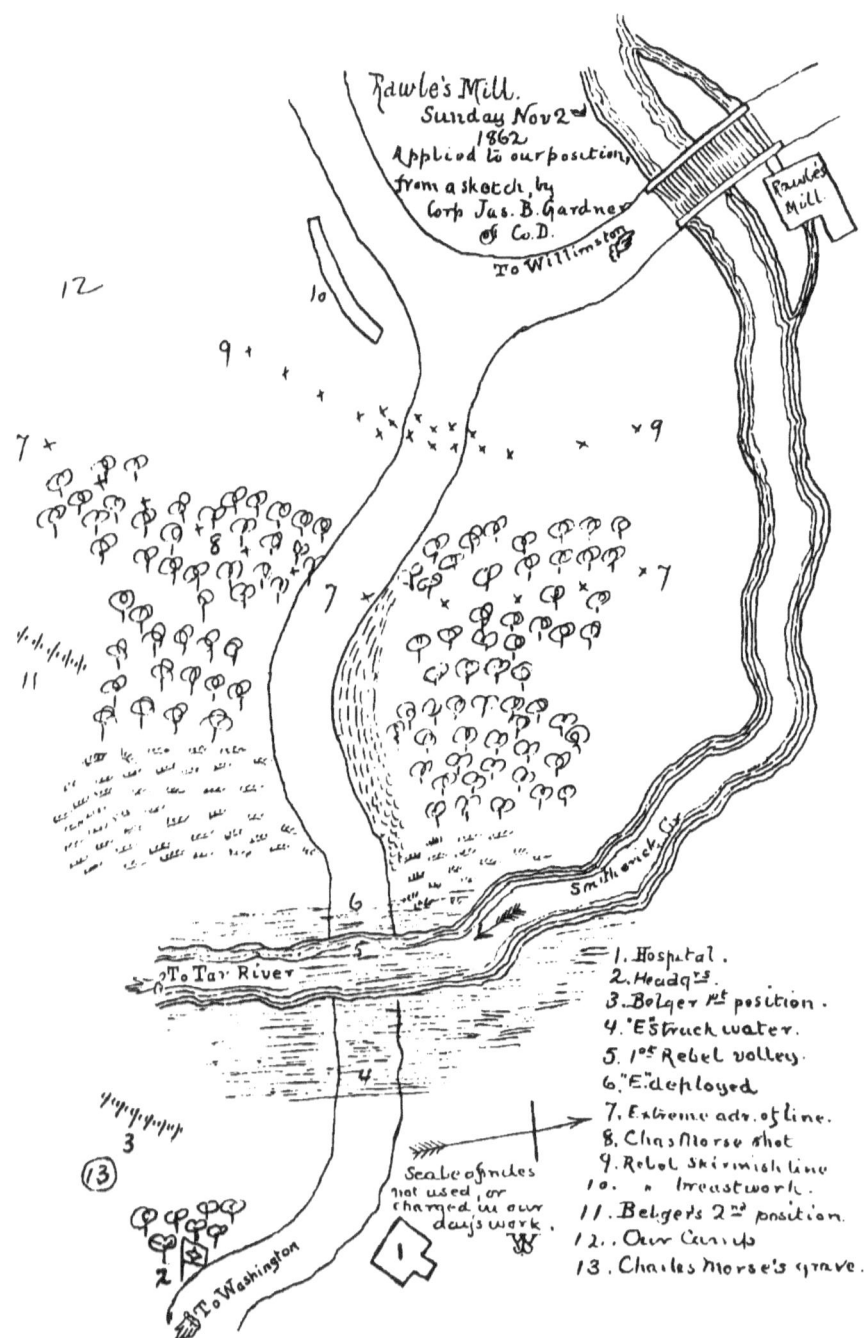

Rawle's Mill.
Sunday Nov 2d
1862
Applied to our positions,
from a sketch, by
Corp Jas. B. Gardner
of Co. D.

To Williamston

To Tar River

Smith creek Cr.

To Washington

Scale of miles
not used, or
changed in our
days work.

1. Hospital.
2. Headqrs.
3. Bolger 1st position.
4. "E" struck water.
5. 1st Rebel volley.
6. "E" deployed
7. Extreme adv. of line.
8. Chas Morse shot
9. Rebel skirmish line
10. " breastwork.
11. Bolger's 2nd position.
12. Our Camp
13. Charles Morse's grave.

just large enough to lie in. A queer-looking camp it was. We have heard to-night that our woollen blankets are to be packed away ; we go in light marching order.

NOVEMBER 1.—Saturday, and of course general cleaning day. So many went into the river before breakfast, and soon found it to be the worst thing possible for us, and expected fever and ague every day till we forgot the circumstance. We had a scare and then a little fun early this morning. Some humorous fellows had fired our nice houses, and fully half the huts in the line were in a blaze; but, instead of trying to stop it, as fast as the boys were smothered out and came to their senses, they "put in a hand," and piled on all the boards they could find. Soon nothing was left of Camp Foster but ashes. Col. Lee would not allow us to appropriate any more lumber, so to-night we will sleep bare-back, excepting our rubber blankets. The portion of the troops who came by land from New Berne having arrived, we start to-morrow—so they say.

NOVEMBER 2.— We started early this morning by the northerly road ; we "fell in" regularly enough, but it was not long before we took the "route step," taking the whole road. A mile or two out we halted and loaded up. Evidently the officers thought there would be plenty of game. We saw or heard little or nothing for about six miles, when we passed a camp-fire, and were told the advance had come across an outpost and killed a man. We still kept up a steady tramp, and about noon the light marching order became heavy again, and whatever useless articles we had on hand were thrown aside. At noon, we halted to feed in a field near a planter's house; the family were all on the piazza. For dinner we had potatoes, chickens, honey, applejack, and persimmons ; the last of which are good if eaten with care, but, if a little green, beware ! We stayed here about an hour, then packed up and started again, followed no doubt by the blessings of that whole family.

RAWLE'S MILL.

About six o'clock (the time probably when our friends at home were writing to us) we heard the artillery, and, coming to a halt, waited anxiously for the next move. To us it soon came. Companies H, Capt. Smith, and C, Capt. Lombard, were ordered forward, "E" being next in line. For a while we heard nothing of them ; but when they were about half-way across the stream the rebels fired into their ranks. They, however, succeeded in crossing, and returned the rebels' fire; but Gen. Foster thought it better to shell them out, so Companies H and C were ordered back ; "H" having Depeyster, Jacobs, and Parker wounded ; and Co. C, Charles Rollins killed ; Sergt. Pond and W. A. Smallidge wounded. Lieut. Briggs was stunned by a shell.

After the return of these companies, Belger's Battery shelled across the stream for some time, trying to dislodge the enemy. Our company and "I" were sent forward in the same track of "H" and "C," Company I being held in reserve. We had the fight all to ourselves. It was quite a distance to the water, and an illimitable one before we arrived on the other side. It was very nearly waist-deep and very cold. We had gone about over, when they fired, but the shot went over our heads: we were nearer than they thought. After coming out and shaking ourselves, Capt. Richardson deployed the company as skirmishers, and we commenced to feel our way up the slope. Before we were well at it we received another volley, which sadly disarranged the ideas of several of us, some of the boys firing back at their flash ; but probably very many of our first volley went nearer the moon than the rebels; and then we jumped for cover. Some found the grape-vines not conducive to an upright position. We got straightened out at last, and gradually worked our way forward ; the writer's position *being in the gutter* (or where the gutter ought to have been) on the left of the road ; soon receiving another volley which we answered in good shape, hoping we did better execution than they had done. We could hear those on the right of the road, but could see nothing, and could only fire on the flash of the rebels. After five or six volleys from our side, and as many from the rebels, we were ordered back, recrossed the ford, and found we had met with loss. Charles Morse was shot through the head. His death must have been instantaneous, as the ball went in very near the temple and came out the opposite side. A detail buried him among the pines, very nearly opposite the surgeon's head-quarters. Charles H. Roberts was quite severely wounded in the left shoulder. There were some narrow escapes, and, among the minor casualties, E. V. Moore was struck by a ball in the heel of his boot ; he was tumbled over ; immediately picked up by the stretcher-bearers and carried to the rear, but would not stay there, and soon found his way to the front again.

The writer, not wishing to be wounded, persistently held his gun ready to ward off all shot, consequently one of the numerous well-aimed shots struck the gun instead of his leg, fracturing the rifle badly; the bullet, after going through the stock of the gun, entered his pantaloons, scraping a little skin from his leg, and finally found its way to his boot.

The surgeon would not report him as wounded or missing, so he had to report back to his company ; found his blanket and tried to turn in, but it was no use: the company had more work on hand.

The part of the company who went into the woods on the right of the road, had a clear passage up the hill, as far as the walking was concerned, but they met their share of fighting, happily coming back with no loss. Parsons, Tucker, and Pierce succeeded in taking three prisoners, who were sent to the rear. We were detailed as baggage guard, which duty we did bravely ! ! Every time the line halted we would lie down, and were asleep as soon as we struck the mud ! ! Finally we made a grand start, forded the stream again, and, after being frightened to death by a stampede of horses up the road, we found a cornfield, and, after forming line several times for practice with the rest of the regiment, spread ourselves on the ground and hugged each other and our wet rubber blankets to get warm.

NOVEMBER 3.— At four o'clock this morning "all was wrong." We were aroused from the most miserable attempt at sleep our boys ever dreamed of trying. It was a mercy to awaken us; only we were so stiff, sore, cold, and hungry, that it was most impossible to get up at all. We were covered with dirt and frost. Our guns were in fearful condition, and we were ordered to clean them and be ready for the road in half an hour. That was good; no chance to eat anything or clean up ourselves; but such is the luck of war. At six A.M. we started on our second day's tramp. Had you asked any of the company, they would have said, "We have been tramping a week." Our colonel gave us a good word this morning, in passing, saying we had done well. We are satisfied; for although "Rawle's Mill" was not an extensive affair, but very few men being engaged, it was an ugly encounter for raw material, fired upon, as we were, while up to our waists in water ; the unknown force of the enemy, apparently on top of the hill, under cover, and having a perfect knowledge of the "lay of the land."

After a steady march of about twelve miles, we entered Williamston, where we halted, broke ranks, and had a *picked-up* dinner, and made ourselves comfortable for two hours or so. Williamston is a pretty little town on the Roanoke. We foraged considerably; most every man having something. The gunboats here effected a junction with us, bringing extra rations, &c.

We visited the wounded, calling on Charley Roberts, who was hit last night. He looks pretty white, but is doing well, and will probably be sent to New Berne on one of the boats. A few of us found a piano in one of the houses, and after moving it to the piazza, Ned Ramsay played, and we sang home tunes for a while, having a large audience on the lawn. Soon after the officers broke up our fun, by "Fall in E," and as that was what we came for, we "fell in," and recommenced our walk at three P.M., marching about five miles, when we pitched camp for the night. Parsons has been made sergeant for his coolness and bravery in taking prisoners.

NOVEMBER 4.—We started early this morning, steadily tramping till a little after noon, when we entered the town of Hamilton, the rebs leaving as our advance went in.

Here we made a long halt, as the men were sore, sick, and lame, as well as tired and hungry. Surgeon Ware made an examination here, and as it was as far as the transports could be with us, he decided to send back what men had succumbed. Our company had two. The unfortunates were put aboard a miserable tub of a boat, with about two hundred sick men on her, and sleeping room for about fifty; but after nearly five days on the crowded, ill-ventilated, poorly provisioned craft, we arrived at New Berne on Sunday morning, Nov. 9th, marched to the old camp-ground, and were received by the guard whom we left there. They washed us, and put us to bed, and then took care of us till we were on our feet again. We had good quarters in the surgeon's tent, and only worried for fear the regiment would come home in the dark, and catch us napping in the officers' quarters.

Rumors are abundant to the effect that the regiment is cut to pieces, but no work for the sick ones, so we write letters by the dozen, smoke, and tell stories of our campaign to the camp-guard. But the company must be looked up.

They started from Hamilton about seven P.M., of the 4th, marching through town with fireworks. Many of the buildings were in flames, having been fired in retaliation, our men being shot at from the houses. Others say the town was burned because a rebel picket shot one of our soldiers on the outskirts of the town. If that was so, it was a wrong done to private property.

NOVEMBER 5. — The camp last night was about four or five miles from Hamilton, in a cornfield as usual. To-day they tramped until noon, going about twelve miles; lunched, then branched off heading towards Tarboro.

NOVEMBER 6. — The main body marched until the small hours of morning, through a drenching rain and a desolate swamp, in the direction of Halifax, before they found a decent camp.

It was a surprise to all ; but instead of going to Tarboro, as was expected, the troops made a backward movement, and the story was, that there was a large force at Tarboro, who intended to attack us and destroy our usefulness. They did not succeed. A portion of the command who marched all night of the 5th on the other road, joined the regiment this forenoon only to find they must keep on the dreary tramp all day and well into the night again before they could reach Hamilton, where they took possession of the houses that were not burned.

NOVEMBER 7. — This morning the ground was covered with snow, adding to the beauties of the marching, which was soon commenced, and continued to Williamston. Here the boys stayed until Sunday, waiting to recruit their strength, and, it was said, to meet transports, but none came ; so they started again, and Sunday night encamped a few miles from Plymouth. Monday they embarked on the "Geo. Collins," bound for New Berne.

NOVEMBER 12. — The camp at New Berne was aroused by the long-roll, by an attack at the bridge, where the pickets are posted. All our guard were called out. Two men of the 24th M. V. were killed. The affair was short, but disturbed the camp for the rest of the night. Our barracks are all done, and we will occupy them as soon as the regiment gets home.

ARRIVAL HOME AGAIN.

NOVEMBER 14. — By the loud cheering and blowing off of steam in the direction of New Berne, we knew the boys had arrived. The regiment reached camp about noon, and a dirtier, more used-up set of men we never saw. Our friends at home would hardly recognize us as the same party who three short weeks before were parading at Readville. But we are now "vets," of one fight — "Rawle's Mill," which we are bound to carry, and as we cannot get it on our flag, the smokers have engraved it on their pipes.

We occupied our barracks to-day. They are new and roomy, but built of green lumber, consequently will soon be well ventilated. The bunks are better and more commodious than those at Readville. Three double ones in each tier ; the cook-room in the centre, with fireplace on one side and room for the sergeants opposite.

November 15.—To-day we were inspected by Gen. Foster, an all-day duty, as we were on our feet from early morning till late in the afternoon. The most important feature of the inspection (to one at least of the company) was the presentation to him of his shattered gun by Gen. Foster, with the permission to "Send it home as a present from your general." It was a relic second to none.

November 20.—We have enjoyed three days of furlough, with no drill or duty to speak of, and most of the company are in good trim again. It has rained much lately, which shuts us in-doors, most of our time being occupied in writing and sleeping. We have just received our blankets, which we left at Washington, never expecting to see them again. They are very acceptable, as the nights are not of the mildest.

Our camp is very pleasantly located, a few rods nearer the Neuse than our first one. The barracks are formed in two wings, with cook-house in rear of each company, and quartermaster's department to be built in the square behind; the line officers in barracks by themselves on each flank, and staff in front of the right wing; the guard line being just outside of all, giving us a convenient parade ground. About six men are drawn from the company each day for camp guard and two for police, making that duty comparatively light; but other work comes in regular order, so we don't have much leisure time. Our routine is about as follows: Reveille at half-past six A.M. and roll-call; then basins to the front, and we go to the water, although we often find some running back to the barracks to get a little more sleep; breakfast, seven; surgeon's call, half-past seven; about this time the first sergeant makes his morning report; guard mounting at eight; then squad drilling from half-past eight till ten, unless the officers get tired of it; company drill, eleven to twelve; then one hour for dinner; company drill from one to two; battalion drill, three to four; company parade and roll-call at half-past four; dress parade, five; supper, six; tattoo and roll-call, half-past seven; taps, half-past eight. No rest for the weary, for between whiles Sergt. Thayer wants three men to get rations, or Sergt. Parsons wants one to sweep barracks, or perhaps the captain wants one to carry a loaded knapsack in front of his quarters for an hour or so for discipline. We wish the paymaster would come; we have been borrowing and lending to each other just to be able to remember the looks of a dollar. There is about three months' pay due us, which would alleviate our misery much just now, especially as Thanksgiving is near at hand.

November 27.—Thanksgiving was a great day in the barracks and a fine day outside, except for those who are on guard. We will recollect them all day, having great pity, but unable to relieve them.

To-day has been talked about and worked up for a week. Turkeys and the fixings have been at a premium, but they say our dinner is safe. The day opened splendidly; just cold enough to induce the boys to play at foot and base ball; some of the officers taking hold and seemingly enjoying the sport.

We had dinner at one P.M. The table, extended nearly the length of the barracks, was covered with our rubber blankets, white side uppermost, looking quite home-like. Our plates and dippers were scoured till we could see our faces in them, and how we hated to rub them up! for, according to tradition, the blacker the dipper and the more dents it had, the longer and harder the service. But it had to be, and was done, and we had to acknowledge "How well it looks!" When we were seated, about a man to every ten was detailed as carver; and a few of us who had engineered to get near the platters were caught and had to cut up and serve. We tried in vain to save a nice little piece or two for ourselves; each time we did it some one would *reach* for it. At last we cut the birds into quarters and passed them indiscriminately. After the meats we had genuine plum-pudding, also nuts, raisins, &c. After the nuts and raisins were on a few made remarks, but the climax was capped by our Lieut. Cumston, who, after telling us not to eat and drink too much, said, "There is a man in camp from Boston, getting statistics; among others, wishes to find out how many of 'E' smoke." The lieutenant said it would be easier counting to ask the question, "How many did not smoke." Several jumped up proud to be counted; among them a few who did occasionally take a whiff. The joke was soon sprung on them, for when they were well on their feet, Lieut. Cumston remarked that he had a few cigars, not quite a box, and hoped they would go round, but those who did not smoke were not to take any. We had the cigars and the laugh on those who wished to figure in the statistics. It was a big dinner, and we did it justice, and gave the cooks credit for it.

In the evening Company D and ourselves gave a musical and literary entertainment. Our barrack was full, and the audience often applauded the amateurs. The programme was as follows : —

PART I.

Song............ .... "Happy are we to-night, boys "..........................
Declamation.............. "England's Interference ".....F. S. Wheeler (Co. D)
Song....... .... "Oft in the Stilly Night "..........................
Declamation.............. "The Dying Alchemist ".....S. G. Rawson (Co. E)
Readings.......................... "Selections ".........J. W. Cartwright (Co. E)
Song.......................... "Viva L'America " . ...
Declamation........ ... "Spartacus to the Gladiators".....J. Waterman (Co. D)
Declamation............ "The Beauties of the Law ".... .H. T. Reed (Co. E)
"Contraband's Visit,"............................Myers and Bryant (Co. E)
Song........ .... "Gideon's Band." ....

INTERMISSION.

PART II.

Song...................... "Rock me to sleep, mother ".......... ....
Declamation.... "Garibaldi's Entree to Naples ".....G. H. Van Voorhis (Co. E)
Song................. ... "There's music in the air ".......... ....
Imitation of Celebrated Actors............................H. T. Reed (Co. E)
Declamation... "Rienza's Address to the Romans ".. N. R. Twitchell (Co. E)
Old Folks Concert.... ....Father Kemp.
Ending with " Home, Sweet Home," by the audience.

NOVEMBER 28.—We went to bed late last night, but had to get up at the regular time this morning. It was hard work after having had a holiday to strike into the old routine at once. There is nothing ahead now but Christmas, pay-day, Washington's Birthday, or another march to enliven us. We have had a few boxes from home, but hope for more, as yesterday a vessel arrived. Our letters say they are coming. We hope to get them about Christmas time, but will use them if they arrive sooner.

At dress-parade to-night Col. Lee complimented us on our behavior yesterday, and upon the way we celebrated.

NOVEMBER 29.—We had a fine time for a change last night. There was one solitary pudding left over from our Thanksgiving dinner. The boys found out that the sergeants had appropriated it, and after taps went for them. We had hardly turned in, when a tall man (name commencing with R) in the left wing of the barracks, but right wing of the company, tuned up with "Pudding, pudding, who's got the pudding?" A sergeant immediately popped his head out of his room, with "Stop that noise" The man would not stop, and, to make matters worse, others picked it up, and soon the entire lot were yelling for pudding. While we were at it strong, in came Col. Lee; but we did not subside worth a cent. So Capt. Richardson came in, and the men, excepting those who had crawled out the ventilators and through the cook-room, were drawn up in line, and the question put to each and all, "Did you say pudding?" Not being able to find out who started the game, the company was ordered out and drilled a while, while the few who shirked their duty by running, crawled back and went to bed. It was short-lived, but fun while it lasted; but we never found that pudding!

DECEMBER 9.—Since Thanksgiving we have been drill, drill, drilling, the same as at Readville, only, we hope, better. There is very little to write about; there is a sameness about camp-life which renders it ofttimes monotonous. To-day has been a sample of brisker times. We would hardly be recognized as the same boys who have occupied the barracks since Thanksgiving night. Then peace and quietness was in camp, now all is bustle and confusion. A few who fell out on the previous march to Tarboro have been examined and talked to, but most of us were allowed to go again if we would behave. A few who are sick have been detailed to stay behind and care for the barracks and the things we have in them. The rest have been as busy as bees making boxes to pack our extra things in. When that was done to our satisfaction we occupied ourselves in writing home.

DECEMBER 10.—Night came without any move being made, and the usual detail for guard was made to-day. We, unlucky guard, already packed this time, had something to do till we were on the road, while the rest only stayed around waiting for the word.

OUR SECOND MARCH.

DECEMBER 11.—The guard was relieved early, and at seven A.M. we fell into line with the regiment, marching across the town to Fort Totten, where we joined our brigade. We made little progress till nearly noon, when, as we thought, we started, but there were continued hitches somewhere, and we had many chances to stretch ourselves on the ground. We were loaded down this time, carrying blankets and knapsacks, and most of us a change of clothes. About four o'clock we passed the pickets on the Trent road, apparently about a regiment, having a prettily situated entrenched camp, on a small elevation; their posts being about an eighth of a mile farther up the road. Soon after leaving them we encountered the first "obstacle" of the expedition. We kept halting, and then starting a little, and soon found we would probably have to sleep in wet clothes. We had to cross quite a long and deep run of water, but, for a change, were allowed to struggle with the plank at the side of the road; but those who succeeded in keeping their feet on the narrow, slippery timber, were few, but dry, and consequently happy. We saw lights ahead, and supposed we were close to camp, but had to march three miles or so before we turned into a *cornfield* on the left of the road, having marched about fourteen miles. A self-imposed detail of two went back to get water for the mess, and what wood we could find; then made our fire, had supper, and turned in. No good bunks now, but plenty of soft dirt to be tucked up in.

DECEMBER 12.—Called up at six this morning; rather stiff in our joints, but still able to have our beds made. We hear this morning that some one took a couple of prisoners last night.

To-day we marched about eighteen miles, camping at nine P.M. No excitement of any kind all day, except hearing of a number of prisoners being taken. Our camp to-night is in a cotton-field, for a change, on the right of the road. And for novelty we try individual fires. Our mess, of about eight, found plenty of rails, but had to get three lots of water, for as fast as one lot would get hot enough for the coffee some one would hit the rail, and over all would go; spoiling our fire and water too. Finally, by ten o'clock, we managed to get supper; then agreed to take turns watching the fire and our spare rails, which we were afraid we should lose. One of the guards falling asleep, our fire went out, also the balance of our rails; but some one foraged around, finding three good ones, and sat on them till morning, that we might have a warm breakfast.

DECEMBER 13.—Last night the company forager, Russell, nearly lost his life. Having stolen or appropriated a mule, he spent most of his time, while on the march, scouring the neighboring chicken-roosts, and, as usual, came in last evening loaded down, a hoop-skirt pannier on each side of his animal, being distended to its uttermost capacity with good things, from eggs to a side of bacon. The picket where he came on the line happened to be a Dutchman, who understood very little English, and nothing of his duty (not of our regiment), and the mule, caparisoned as he was with the white skirts, stealing upon him with little noise, frightened the poor fellow so that he fired at the forager, *and then challenged him,* but after a deal of talk, our man got by and rendered a good account of himself.

We started about seven this morning, and after marching about nine miles heard firing ahead, and were ordered to halt, and " right and left " was the word. Lying down, we rested while our artillery went through the line. We waited a long time. Then we moved forward, and, entering a large field on the left, were drawn up in line of battle. We were on an elevation, where we could see all that was going on, or thought we could, which served the purpose, as we all found out sooner or later. The men knew little or nothing, and anyone asking an officer, he always replied, " I'm sure I cannot tell you "—a most unsatisfactory way of explaining matters.

About four o'clock we stacked our arms, with orders not to leave the ranks; and supposing the enemy to be in our immediate vicinity, we kept quiet for an hour;

then, as there did not appear to be any special movement, we were allowed to get something to eat; and soon found we were to stay here all night, but were not allowed to remove our accoutrements.

From our position we have a beautiful view of our camp-ground. We are situated on a knoll, with General Stevenson's head-quarters in our immediate vicinity, with the different regiments scattered in all directions ; while down in the woods, directly in front of our line, we can just see the cavalry picket. We are wondering if all our fighting is to be done on Sundays. Our first fight was on Sunday, and it is now Saturday night ; and we are so close to the enemy that we have orders to sleep with our rifles in our hands. Probably no baked beans or brown bread for us to-morrow.

KINSTON.

December 14.—Sunday morning opened finely ; and after a quiet night we were up bright and early, starting at half-past seven for another day's tramp, which we are in good condition to do, having rested well yesterday. This is our fourth day from New Berne, and by the road we marched it is a considerably longer distance than by the Neuse Road, whch, it is rumored, is heavily barricaded, and would have delayed us much.

We marched pretty steadily till about nine o'clock, when we heard firing ahead ; and the artillery of our brigade went through the lines at double quick. Then we were drawn up in line in a field at the right of the road, piling up our knapsacks and leaving a man or two to guard them. We had an idea there was fighting ahead of us, but thought it quite a way off, until a few shells whistled unpleasantly near. Soon we had orders, " Forward !" We entered a swamp where we saw a number of the 45th M. V. wounded and many dead. Guns, knapsacks, and accoutrements scattered in all directions. It almost beggared description. Col. Lee was leading the way : our duty was to follow. We would have preferred going *round that swamp*. And such a place to drop in ! Anyone shot there, took a chance of being drowned also. Up to our hips in water ; strangled or tripped up by the grape-vines. Sometimes two would jump for the same hummock, and, stiking midway, both would drop into the water. It was our " Slough of Despond ;" and we were expecting each minute to receive a volley, and be served as the other regiments had been, but we were agreeably disappointed. There was plenty of shot and shell which went over our heads. When we were clear of the swamp we could see a building on top of the hill. It turned out to be a church. We arrived there just in time to see two or three hundred rebels being led to the rear, and another lot just coming in with a flag of truce. Our forces also captured a battery which the rebels could not carry off. We went back on the road to get our knapsacks, and then took our position in line. While waiting to move on, we saw a lot of muskets and rifles piled up beside the road. A splendid double-barrel gun took the eye of many, but it looked heavy, so it was left.

The enemy did not succeed in burning the bridge, although it was loaded with tar and cotton. The man detailed for this work started the fire, but probably his clothes, becoming saturated with spirits, took fire, as when we crossed we saw him lying in the mud under the bridge, badly burned and dead. The cotton was thrown overboard and the bridge saved.

We crossed about two o'clock p.m. After passing a formidable looking water-battery, just at the right of the bridge, we marched about two miles to Kinston, which was deserted, except by the darkies and occasionally a poor white. At the junction of the streets cotton was piled up and on fire,—a great waste of batting, but they probably thought it would impede our progress. If it had been the cause of the destruction of the place, Gen. Foster probably would have been blamed. We marched across the town, and while we saw most of the regiments bivouacking and getting their supper, we kept on about a mile, to drive the rebels from a hill from which they could shell the place. After losing two hours, we counter-marched, camping close to the railroad station and a large corn elevator, where we had a good supper ; after which, instead of turning in, some of us started on a "lark." We went throught the post-office and other buildings, but were finally driven back by the cavalry. After visiting the corn elevator, which was on fire, and filling our canteens with water for morning, we tore down a fence back of the station, making some very nice beds, and turned in.

DECEMBER 15.—After turning in last night it was impossible to sleep, the cause being the music of a band farther down the railroad track. It was a serenade to the general, probably, but we took it all in. Our batteries had been practising all the evening on the hill occupied by the rebels, altogether making it lively, but conducive to sleep.

At half-past four this morning we were aroused by the usual drum-beat, ate breakfast, and started once more; and as we had more resting than fighting yes-terday, we were in a comparatively good condition, marching out of Kinston in good spirits. We crossed the river by the same bridge where the fight occurred, and, after burning it, took the road towards Goldsboro. Nothing worthy of note turned up to-day but our toes and heels alternately, which did not interest us much. After a steady march of sixteen miles, we encamped in a *cornfield* on the right of the road. (About all the fields we ever did camp in were cornfields.) We would have liked a potatoe-patch or dry cranberry meadow for a change, but probably Col. Lee or the exigencies of the case demanded a cornfield. If the colonel had been obliged to have slept once across the rows of these or between them, filled as they oftentimes were with water, he would have picked out other quarters without doubt. This camp is about five miles from a place called White-hall, where they say we are to "catch it."

DECEMBER 16.—Another hard night ; one of a few very cold and disagreeable ones. We left the ranks early for rails, and after carrying them two or three miles, found, on arriving at camp, there were plenty on hand and not accounted for. We got our supper and tried to s'eep, but it was almost impossible. We would have suffered severely had it not been for our woollen blankets; as it was, when we woke up this morning, many of us found the water in our canteens frozen, said canteens having been used as pillows during the night.

WHITEHALL.

After starting at seven o'clock, we kept halting continually until nine. We had travelled not more than four or five miles when we heard heavy firing in our immediate front. Our brigade being ahead, our regiment was sent in about the first. We left the main road, taking the one over the hill on the left, and were immediately under fire. Here we came upon two men of "A" who had been killed by a shot or shell. We dropped our knapsacks and filed along a line of fence, coming to a halt in front of the Neuse, with the rebels on the opposite shore.

We fired several volleys by company, then the order came, "At will," which was easier. We had an old rail-fence in front, and beyond that a few barrels of pitch or turpentine, then a slope, and the water, and the rebels beyond. We received a good share of their bullets, and hoped ours did better execution, as we were fortunate in not losing a man. There were several narrow escapes, however. The flag was immediately behind our company, and a part of the time the flag of the 9th New Jersey was unfurled behind us also, which might have drawn an extra amount of fire; but we did not suffer any loss, while some of the companies lost several. "A," four killed and seven wounded; "B," one wounded; "C," three killed; "K," one killed; "D," two wounded; "F," one wounded; "G," two wounded; "H," two wounded. We were on the rebels' right. We stayed there about an hour and a half and then were ordered back, and started directly across the field in line of fire for cover, where we could see other regiments flat on the ground. All the protection we had there, was by hugging mother earth and folding our arms back of our heads, the bullets whistling close to us in a neighborly fashion. Here we waited, and those who had hard-tack munched it; but we kept up a thinking all the while whether the muscles of our arms would stop a bullet from going through our heads. Soon Belger's battery took our old place and opened on the rebels, who treated them pretty severely for a time, as we could see good R. I. material dropping constantly. The battery boys came for the water we had in our canteens, with which to cool their guns, the firing having been quite brisk. After two hours of very steady work, the rebels concluded to give up the fight. As they had destroyed the bridge yesterday, we could not chase them, so fell in and started again for Goldsboro, and about eight o'clock camped in a field at the junction of two roads.

GOLDSBORO.

December 17. — There was no time this morning to cook coffee, so we started on a cold-water breakfast, after another cold night, with little good sleep, and marched without incident until four P.M., when we heard the usual cannonade at the front. As soon as the noise of the cannon was heard, then commenced the usual straggling. All have some of course. The attention of our boys was called to a scene upon which we looked with surprise, and which many of our company will never forget. As we passed from the main road to take position on the hill, we saw a man, or what was dressed as a man, in Uncle Sam's clothes, importuned by another to join his command. He would not budge ; and the concluding words we heard as we passed by, were : "Damn it, man! just look here : look at this regiment going in ; there is not a *man* there ; they are all *boys* with no hair on their faces,—and *you afraid!*" We pitied the fellow, and often wondered if he joined his company. His pride had evidently gone on a furlough. We halted on a high hill, from which we could see all that was going on, and soon found we were in reserve, which pleased us all. After getting turnips and sweet potatoes,—of which we found a plenty (all planted for us),—we straggled to the edge of the bluff and watched the fight. In a tree close to where we stood was a signal station, and by that we supposed Gen. Foster was near. On the left we could see the railroad which leads into Goldsboro, and the fighting over it; to the right, the bridge ; while in front, close to the river, there seemed to be a continuous sheet of flame from our advance and the rebels. Some of our men worked their way to the mill ; and a story was told by one of the 17th Mass. Vols., who reached the bridge on his own account, that he saw a train of cars stop there, and, just as it halted, a shot from one of our batteries struck the engine in the head-plate, smashing the engine badly. He could see men jump from the cars in all haste. (This story was told several years after the action; and the fact of those men coming as they did, and perhaps others behind, may have been the reason we left so suddenly, and went to New Berne.)

About seven o'clock Gen. Foster rode past our line, saying : "The object of the expedition [the burning of the bridge and partially destroying the connection between the Gulf States and Richmond] is accomplished. We are going to New Berne."

We were immediately formed, and started on the back track with cheers for the general; but we had not gone three miles before we found we were not "out of the woods." Orders came to countermarch, so we turned about, wondering what all the artillery firing meant. We tramped back about two miles or so through the woods, on fire on both sides of the road, turned to the left down hill, and formed line in silence, waiting. We were not allowed to speak or light our pipes, but waited, it seemed, for two hours. The regiment was formed in division column closed in mass; the company behind us being only a few feet away, and in front nothing but the pickets and supposable rebels. After staying here a while we heard the artillery go along the road, and soon followed. We reached camp about ten o'clock, tired and hungry, but no chance to get anything to eat, and a man missing. He turned up afterwards, having settled himself for a nap when we were in the woods. Not finding any one near when he awakened, he concluded to strike out for himself—happily remembering that old broken caisson beside the road, and recollecting on which side he left it on going in, he soon came "Russelling" into camp with the rest of us.

DECEMBER 18.—We started for home about five this morning, expecting to make easy marches, but have been disappointed so far, as we have tramped just about the same gait as when going up, making about twenty miles to-day and camping in the same field we did the night out of Kinston, about five miles from Whitehall.

DECEMBER 19.—We were up and at it at the usual time this morning, on the home tramp, which kept up the spirits of many. About ten o'clock we came in sight of our first day's fighting ground. We found that several of the graves of our men had been opened by the rebels. After repairing them we kept on, taking the Neuse Road, which we steered clear of in coming up on account of the heavy entrenchments and barricades the rebels had placed on it. Every little while we had to leave the road and take to the woods to get by their obstructions, which continued for four or five miles from Kinston; some of them were very formidable.

About three o'clock we marched into a large field on the left of the road to receive rations, which we understood had been brought to us on the cars from New Berne, and it was about time; our larder was getting low. We received a little bread, but not enough to satisfy both stomach and haversack, so we filled the former and stowed away the crumbs that were left in the latter. The report is that the bread and beef were left at New Berne, and soap and candles shipped to us,—an explanation which did not soothe our feelings entirely.

We marched about five miles farther and then camped for the night.

DECEMBER 20. — After some trouble we managed to get to bed last night about eleven o'clock; but for a long time after that the mules kept us awake; perhaps they were hungry also. The weather was clear and not cold, so we got a little rest. At six o'clock this morning we were ordered on, after a very light breakfast, excepting for a few who may have foraged. There were a few chickens and a little applejack about *our* mess. To-day has been the hardest of any day of the tramp, and there has been more straggling. The company organization was in the line, but thinned out terribly. We had no noon-rest; but at two o'clock we filed from the road to a field, came to the front, and received a good scolding. Our regiment looked as if it had been through two Bull Runs; only about 150 left, and the rest not "accounted for." In fact there were very few left of those who should do the accounting. The colonel stormed a little, but that did not bring up the men; so, as he was probably as hungry, if not as tired, as we were, he let us go to eating, which was a decided farce. Our haversacks were as flat as our stomachs. We found a few grains of coffee and tobacco-crumbs in the bottom of our bags, and succeeded in digging a few sweet potatoes, which we ate raw. We were told they were very *fullsome*. We waited here two hours or so for the stragglers, who finally came along. They had been having a fine time, plenty of room to walk, and two hours more to do it in than we had; and, more than that, they were in the majority, so nothing could be done but "Right shoulder shift" and put the best foot forward. About sundown we saw, in crossing a bridge, a wagon-load of hard-tack bottom side up in the creek. Some of the boys sampled the bread, but it was not fit to eat. Shortly after a signboard indicated fourteen miles to New Berne. That was encouraging! The walking was fearful, the roads full of water, in some places waist deep, and covered with a skimming of ice. At last we met a wagon loaded with bread, and after much talk with the driver we got what we wanted. Next we met a man who said it was only twelve miles to New Berne. They either have long miles or else some one made a mistake ; we seemingly had been walking two hours or more from the fourteenth mile post, and now it was twelve miles. We came to the conclusion not to ask any more questions, but "go it blind."

We at last reached the picket-post,' seven miles out, and halted to rest and allow the artillery to go through. Here Col. Lee told us we were at liberty to stay out and come into camp Sunday ; but most of " E " thought of the letters and the supper we would probably get, and concluded to *stand by the flag.* After a rest we started again, and at last began to close up and halt often, so we knew we were coming to some place or other.

The writer has no very distinct idea of those last seven miles, excepting that he was trying to walk, smoke, and go to sleep at the same time, and could only succeed in swearing rather faintly, and in a stupid sort of manner, at everything and every one. It was dark and foggy, but finally we saw what appeared to be the headlight of a locomotive a long way off. Then the fort loomed up, and we were passing under an arch or bridge, and in a few minutes we reached "E's" barrack, and our troubles were all forgotten. Now we were wide awake ; gave three hearty cheers for every one ; had all the baked beans and coffee we could stagger under ; and then the captain's " Attention for letters " brought us to our feet. Some had as many as a dozen. They had to be read at once, and, notwithstanding our fatigue and the lateness of the hour, read they were.

CAMP STEVENSON.

DECEMBER 21.—Sunday. A splendid day ; but what a miserable-looking set of boys we are !—stiff, lame, and dirty, and hungry for more beans. We received the welcome order, " No work for three days." We went to church this morning, so there are really only two days and a half, and they will soon be gone. But we have letters to answer, trips down-town to make, for those who can get passes ; and the first thing we know it will be Wednesday.

DECEMBER 24.—Wednesday, and our duties have commenced again : regular camp routine,—drill, guard, and police, the same as before the last march.

We are forgetting the sore feet, and gaining flesh every day, and an occasional run down town to Blagg's tends to rub off the rough edge of being cooped behind sentries.

DECEMBER 25.—Christmas. A fine day, and, being my birthday, I was allowed a furlough, for chum and self, from reveille till tattoo.

We started as early as possible for New Berne, and, among other things, had a first-class turkey dinner, with all the fixings, silverware, cut glass, white table-cloth, and some one to wait on table. But for us, as for all, the day came to a close, and at the usual time we were back, no better than about eighty others, excepting the memory of home-life which the associations of the day had called up.

DECEMBER 30.—The paymaster looked in on us. He is the first we have had any dealings with, and we are glad he came, for most of "E" have been "hard up." We received pay from August 29th to November 1st,—$27.30 each. We expected to get the whole, and were disappointed ; for when many of us squared up, it took about all that we received to settle our debts. We are drilled now as a brigade nearly every day, firing blank cartridges ; consequently our guns need extra cleaning, and we get more marching. Evidently they mean our brigade to be number one.

DECEMBER 31.—The last day of an eventful year to us, but the matters worthy of note are few and far between.

We drilled hard from two o'clock till we had barely time to clean up for dress parade, and very little can be said of brigade drills in their favor. The principal thing being, we passed the "defile" many times, and formed *en echelon*, about all the afternoon. It may be it was to celebrate the new "star,"—our Gen. Stevenson wearing his for the first time to-day. If that was it we will forgive him, but if the star is going to increase the brigade drills we shall wish he never had won it.

Our brigade now is the 2d in the 1st Division, Acting Major-General Wessels, and is composed of the 5th R. I., 10th Conn., 24th Mass., 44th Mass., and Belger's R. I. Battery.

1863.

JANUARY 1.—To-day we were mustered for two months' pay, and of course we were happy till our ardor was cooled by our captain, who told us it might be *three months* before we received our money . All the consolation to us is, our names are on the list. Our barracks are up in arms, as we are getting ready for the entertainment this evening. Those who are not practising or ordering round are working like beavers putting things to rights.

JANUARY 2.—We had a good time last evening; everything went off smoothly, the parts being well taken by boys from the different companies. The following is the programme : —

SECOND

DRAMATIC AND MUSICAL ENTERTAINMENT

BY THE

44TH REGIMENTAL DRAMATIC ASSOCIATION.

———

Prologue	H. T. Reed.
Overture	Band.
Recitation	F. D. Wheeler.
Song	Quartette Club.
Recitation	C. A. Chase.
Recitation	E. L. Hill.

BAND.

TRIAL SCENE FROM "MERCHANT OF VENICE."

Shylock	H. T. Reed.
Duke	W. Howard.
Antonio	D. F. Safford.
Bassanio	F. D. Wheeler.
Gratiano	J. H. Waterman.
Portia	L. Millar.
Solanio	F. A. Sayer.

BAND.

GRAND MINSTREL SCENE.

Opening Chorus	Company.
Louisana Lowlands	H. Howard.
Dolly Day	F. A. Sayers.
Shells of the Ocean	H. Howard.
Susianna Simpkins	F. A. Sayers.
Ham Fat Man	J. H. Myers.

Concluding with

A TERRIBLE CATASTROPHE ON THE NORTH ATLANTIC R.R.

With Characters by the Company.

___

Director	H. T. Reed.
Assistant Manager	D. F. Safford.
Secretary	W. Howard.
Treasurer	J. M. Waterman.

EXECUTIVE COMMITTEE.

F. D. Wheeler, L. Millar and F. A. Sayers.

___

JANUARY 5.—In writing up the events of January 1st, including the "Catastrophe," characters by the company, we did not think we were on the brink of an actual one. It seems Col. Lee thought our captain just the officer to take charge of the new ambulance corps, a larger command, and a very responsible one ; but the captain thought of the matter overnight, and has decided to stay with the boys whom he enlisted, many of them entering " E " because *he was to be captain.*

JANUARY 8. — We have had several cases of fever lately, occasioned, it is said, by malaria from the lower swamps in the neighborhood. We have one slough close by us, between our barracks and the river. At first we tried to fill it up, but finding it apparently had no bottom, gave it up, and now use it to empty our swill into, keeping it constantly stirred up, of course. Our camp is on as high and dry ground as any in the neighborhood, but there is evidently something about it which is wrong.

We are now also having the benefit of the rainy season, consequently most of our drill is in-doors. We like it for a change, as it gives us more leisure to write; and I fear we are getting fearfully lazy, as we do a great deal of sleeping. It is about time to give us another march or we will get rusty. The rain still reigns, and we probably will not move till it is over.

Just about this time look out for quinine. We are ordered to take it every night to kill the fever. Our captain looks out for us, that we do not lose our share. Generally, Sergeant Thayer goes round with the big bottle, giving each man his dose, the captain following close by. Several have tried various ways to dodge it, but they were too sharp for us, and when they caught us we had to take a second glass of it. We would give ours up if we thought there was not enough to go through the officers' tents ; but they *say* they take their dose *after us*. We are afraid it is a long time after.

JANUARY 12.—We are having another kind of excitement to-day. Boxes are flooding the barracks ; the "Express" and "Torpedo" having brought about one box to each man. We appreciate the good things, but acknowledge there is more sickness after having received them ; still we "cry for more." It was reported we could smoke on guard at night. We revelled in the privilege, when lo ! all too soon, came the word, "No smoking ;" and it turned out to be a hoax ; but it was thoroughly enjoyed by the boys.

Rumors of war and another expedition are floating around. A number of regiments have had their twelve hours' notice, some say to Wilmington, others Charleston, but it is safe to say the majority do not know ; so all we have to do is to wait patiently, and by and by we may find ourselves gone.

There has been a raid towards Trenton, and it is supposed that "they accomplished the object," &c.

JANUARY 21.—Last night our neighbors "D" gave the affair of the season, the occasion being marred only by the lack of ladies, which was in part supplied by several of the boys dressing up in clothes borrowed from the colored ladies down town.

The following card explains itself : —

GRAND BALL.

SIR,

The pleasure of your company, with ladies, is respectfully solicited at a Grand Ball to be held in the Grand Parlor of the Fifth Avenue Hotel (No. 4 New Berne), on Tuesday Evening, January 20th, 1863.

The management beg leave to state that nothing will be left undone on their part to make it *the* party of the season.

MANAGERS.

C. H. Demeritt.   W. Howard.   J. E. Leighton.

ORDER OF DANCES.

1.	Sicilian Circle	March to Tarboro.
2.	Quadrille	New England Guard.
3.	Polka Quadrille	Kinston Galop.
4.	Quadrille	Yankee Doodle.

Waltz, Polka, Redowa, Scottische.

5.	Quadrille	Bloody 44th Quickstep.
6.	Les Lanciers	Connecticut 10th March.
7.	Quadrille	Lee's March.
8.	Contra (Virgina Reel) . . .	Rebel's Last Skedaddle.

I cannot write much of a description of this affair, except to say it was enjoyable, and the hall crowded. A cousin of mine, in the 39th Ill. Infantry, is on a visit from Norfolk, and of course we had to go to the dance. Soon after entering, as we stood looking on, I placed my hand on the shoulder of the man in front, and, slightly leaning upon him, remarked, "A gay sight!" "Yes, it is," in a voice perfectly recognizable. I turned my head to be sure of what I had been doing, begged his pardon, and changed base instantly, carrying Ned to the farthest possible limit of the hall. It was Col. Lee I had been so familiar with, and all the time I was conspiring to break a rule, in having a man sleep in camp who did not belong there, although this was an extra occasion; and I suppose more than one mess had an extra member that night.

JANUARY 22.— The rain is continuous : over a week now of steady weather, and nothing but inside drills, under Lieut. Newell, who is always trying, and generally succeeds, to "PUT IN MORE SNAP, MEN!" interspersed with bayonet drills on our own hook, and occasionally, when it holds up for a few hours, Col. Lee stretches our legs with a drill outside.

At dress parade lately the order was read directing the following victories to be inscribed upon the flags of the regiments, batteries, &c., which were on the Goldsboro expedition : —

KINSTON, DECEMBER 14, 1862.

WHITEHALL, DECEMBER 16, 1862.

GOLDSBORO, DECEMBER 17, 1862.

On account of the resignation of Captains Lombard and Reynolds, the rank of Capt. Richardson is advanced, he becoming third. Consequently "E" is color company, a position not only of honor to the captain and his men, but in some positions in which we may be placed it means dangerous work. We hope we may carry them well, and when we give them up either to some other company or when we are disbanded, it will be with the same pride that we take them now.

Several of the company are a little under the weather, but no fever cases yet. We have been fortunate, while other companies are having quite a number of sick men.

January 25.—As we proposed having a dance soon after "D," and there are such strong rumors of movements of troops floating about camp, we made up our minds not to lose our chance, and had it last night. Those who attended were highly gratified. The notices, posted on the different barrack-doors, read as follows :—

BAL-MASQUE.

A grand Regimental Bal-Masque will be held to-night, January 24th, at the Barracks of Company E. None admitted except *commissioned officers* and those *en costume.*

There was a full house, notwithstanding the restrictions, and we had a fine time. Several were dressed as ladies, and made passably good-looking ones, Miss Rawson, of Boston, and Miss Emerson, of Waltham, carrying off the honors. Most of our officers called upon us, bringing a few of the 10th Conn.

January 28.—Another spell of weather. It has rained constantly for two days, with no intermission. Some of the regiments have been moved. The 24th Mass., 10th Conn., and 5th R. I., have gone ; but we still stay behind, probably intended for some sort of a tramp. Lieut. Cumston goes on this expedition, and may see some tall fighting at Charleston while we are doing police and camp. guard duty ! But as he is of " E," we will take the credit of Charleston, and put it on our pipes beside the rest. We gave him six rousing cheers, and a hand. shake as he went by the barracks to join his command.

Several Boston gentlemen have been here, some stopping with our officers,— among them Mr. J. G. Russell, father of Geo. Russell, of our company,—but they have all moved down town, and we hear that when some of them undertook to leave for Boston, Col. Messinger, the Provost Marshal, would not let them start, on account of the movement of troops.

PLYMOUTH.

February 1.—Sunday, and another move at last. We left the barracks about seven o'clock this morning, marched through the town and aboard the " Northerner," by far the most commodious steamer we have been on since we came out. There are awful stories of her having been condemned, and, as a last resort, sold to government for transporting troops. There is plenty of room however ; so, as we cannot help it, we content ourselves, and hunt around for our stateroom. Our party was lucky enough to get one, seven of us occupying it ; and after a good dinner we turned in, as we had seen all there was to be seen on the river before, and did not know how soon we would be called upon to lose sleep. We steamed at a good rate down the Neuse, and at dark were still at sea. We are having a good time so far ; not overcrowded, the vessel clean, and plenty of good stuff to eat, as we had just received boxes by the " Fry," chartered by our friends at home. There was a box for every man, and in some cases two, so our knapsacks and haversacks are filled with home-made eatables, instead of govern- ment meat and bread. We have our band with us, so many expect some good times. The band takes two good fellows from "E,"—Park and Ramsay; and all the consolation we get for the loss is an extra onion now and then, and perhaps a little less noise in the barracks from Ned.

FEBRUARY 2.—Passed Roanoke on our right, about eight o'clock this morning; sea smooth and weather pleasant. Had a good breakfast of dried beef and water. We entered Roanoke river for the second trip on it about noon, and after about four hours' pleasant sail we were alongside the wharf at Plymouth. Since we were here in November the town has become sadly demoralized. The rebels entered it one fine day and drove what troops were there into the Custom House, and then set fire to the place, destroying the larger part. It is decided not to disembark the regiment till to-morrow. The cooks are ashore somewhere, and are making our coffee, while we are lounging round on deck and through the vessel, having a free and easy time, or located in some cosey nook writing up.

FEBRUARY 3.—Last night was a holiday time. We had dancing on the vessel, and "the band played." This morning was ushered in with a slight change. The ground was covered with snow, and everything had a decidedly Northern outlook, some of the companies came ashore to-day, and are quartered in a granary owned by one J. C. Johnston. We were somewhat crowded on the vessel, but would gladly sacrifice the room for the heat, as it is very cold here. Our company is in the second story, and most all are in their blankets trying to keep warm, as there is no chance to have fires in the building. Athough the town is provost guarded, most anyone can roam round by dodging the officers and sentries. About all our rations, so far, have been obtained away from company quarters, many preferring a change. We find quite a number of natives here; one, for instance, John Fenno, a unionist, was drafted into the rebel service, deserted, ran to our lines, and joined the native cavalry regiment (Buffaloes), and consequently is in a bad predicament. He will have to fight to the death; for if he is taken the rebels will hang him. He is now with his family; but when the town is deserted by the troops, he is liable, with the rest, to another raid such as they had a few weeks ago.

FEBRUARY 4.—We are having an easy time so far, excepting for the cold weather. We have no guard or drill as yet; a part of the 27th M. V. do provost duty. There are rumors of a regimental guard, around our quarters; so all who could cleared out early and stayed all day. A party of us visited the court-house, prison, and graveyard. All but the last, with a church close by, show marks of being used as targets. After picking ivy from the graveyard wall, to send home, we started out of town on a private scout. About a mile's walk brought us to a picket; who thought our visit farther had better be indefinitely postponed; so, after a pleasant chat with them, whom we found to be natives, deserters from the rebel army, and, of course, unionists, we took the "right about" and tramped towards camp arriving just in time for inspection and dress parade at half-past four P.M.

FEBRUARY 5.—Had a ball in our old granary last night. Some who were to go on guard to-day turned in early, and all we know of it is, that those who went had a good time.

Our regiment is to help the 27th in their guard-duty. Our guard-house is a grocery store, close to the granary, and the duty is very light. It rained about all day, and the snow is consequently gone, leaving the roads in a fearfully bad condition.

HAM FAT.

FEBRUARY 7.—Freedom of the town for to-day, and all over town we went ; had a dug-out race, and about all who were in it got a ducking. Our party went up the shore of the river some distance. We saw the ways where a ram had been started, but was destroyed to keep our gunboats from taking her. We then branched off into the woods and finally found a picket-post, where we got some good cider and had a chat, arriving home just in time to get our guns and "fall in."

It seemed our right wing was "on a march." Quartermaster Bush said we were going for wood, but we could not understand why it took four or five companies to escort an equal number of wagons a few miles from town, unless there was a large force of the enemy about ; and if there was, why had we heard nothing from them for five days? Our orders were "light marching order," nothing but guns and ammunition; but most of "E" took haversacks and dippers, and were glad we did. We started about two o'clock this afternoon, and after marching about two miles we struck an "obstacle." The road was completely barricaded by large trees felled across it ; and as cutting would delay us the rest of the day, we turned into the woods and went through a swamp, and soon found ourselves in the road again, marching towards "Long Acre." We left "B" and "C" at the junction of two roads, near a blacksmith shop. We soon left the wagons also, they probably stopping for the wood which was piled up by the roadside. We still kept "marching on," and by dark we were tired as well as hungry. There was worse for us in store, however. The boys ahead began to scatter and growl, and soon we were in the water. It was icy-cold and waist deep. Some tried the runway on the side, but it was slippery with ice. One of the boys made fruitless attempts to keep both feet on the rail. His efforts on that *parallel bar* were edifying ; but being the *youngest member of* "E" (sweet seventeen), he will have more time than the rest of us to improve. After much struggling, down he went, gun and all. The water was three feet deep; and after fishing up his rifle he concluded to wade with us the rest of the way. We know "a thing of beauty is a joy forever." He was not in a beautiful or joyous mood then, but *will* probably be a JOY forever.

The ford seemed to us about a mile long. It was probably only a quarter, if that; but it came to an end at last, and we footed the rest of the way on dry land; varying the monotony by private details for forage at every house we came to ; striving to get ahead of the officers in their attempts to *save* the *cider* from us.

Between ten and eleven o'clock P.M. we halted, and were informed that the "object, &c., was accomplished," "about faced," which brought "E" to the front, and started for home. Twelve of our men went ahead as advance guard, under command of Lieut. Newell, and another twelve of us as support. A short distance behind came the column. We were on the same road, and knew we had the same ford to recross, and suffered torments until it was over with, and we fairly out of its sight. We foraged right and left; hardly a man of us without two or three old hens, dipper full of honey, and a few with a ham or two. The advance and support had the most and fattest pickings of course. We rejoined the other companies, "B" last, at the blacksmith shop; and about five o'clock A M. came in sight of the picket and saw Plymouth.

FEBRUARY 8.—Then Lieut. Newell told us to "go," and we went, as well as we could, for quarters. Arriving at the granary, and having left our *chickens* at a negro shanty to be cooked, we turned in, all booted and muddy, and slept through everything till nearly noon. When we started up for breakfast it was a comical sight. Nearly all had turned in in their wet clothes, and of course were about as wet when they got up, and very stiff. We found our chickens and ate them. While eating, the 27th guard called us, saying the regiment was under orders and we were to leave immediately. The way those chickens disappeared made those darkies laugh. We went back happy, as we knew when once on board the steamer we could sleep for a while and get rested; for after being on an all-night march of twenty-five miles at least, we were tired out, and felt we would be safer from another trip, for a day or two, than if on shore. We were all on board by half-past four o'clock, and soon after dropped down stream, leaving Plymouth and the 27th in all their glory. The boys who had bunks coming up are forbidden that pleasure *now*, so a dozen of us congregated together on the deck, outside the cabin, with shelter tents tacked up as roofs; and we think we are having a better time than those inside, and no "sour grapes" in the mess either.

FEBRUARY 9.—We managed to get clear of the Roanoke river some time in the night, but ran aground in the Sound at noon, thinking we were opposite Roanoke, but did not reach there till nearly night, when the officers went on shore, while the steamer took on coal. The steamer which came out to us here was the "Halifax," recognized by many as the boat which was formerly on Charles river at home as a pleasure boat. She brought rumors of defeat at New Berne, and that we could not get up the river, so were going to Charleston, or Fort Munroe and the Potomac. But we kept on in the direction of Brant Isle and New Berne' just the same.

FEBRUARY 10.—We have had nothing of interest to-day, except a very pleasant sail up the river, once in a while shooting at ducks; but the officers soon stopped that fun. We arrived at New Berne about four o'clock in the afternoon, crossed the long bridge, marched through the city, and are once more in our old barracks.

CAMP STEVENSON AGAIN.

FEBRUARY 11.—Drill, drill, all day, for a change. Our band has received the new pieces from Boston, and is now expected to shine. Among our many visitors from home is ex-Sergeant Wheelwright who came out on the schooner "Fry." He went on the Plymouth or "Ham Fat" tramp, and took to foraging naturally. He stole a mule the first thing, but had to give it up to an officer. Next we saw him on a horse, which he managed to keep. He does not take kindly to quinine or hard-tack; he likes the colonel's fare better. It is a mere matter of taste, though! There is not much doing, except drilling and trying each day to be the cleanest company, as then we get off guard for twenty-four hours, the greatest inducement that could be offered us. We have succeeded in being both the dirtiest and cleanest. At the first inspection we thought we were clean, but a mouldy milk-can condemned us, and we had to furnish double guard, but since then have carried off the honors once or twice.

FEBRUARY 21.—The time for the last two weeks has been used up with drill, quinine, and getting ready for the ball last night. It was ahead of anything yet. The partition between " D " and " E " was taken down, and about all day spent in fixing up our hall. The bunks were hidden by the shelter-tents festooned, and scrolls underneath, with the names of the officers on them. The card of the managers was as follows :—

GRAND MASQUERADE BALL.

Sir,

The pleasure of your company, with ladies, is respectfully solicited at a Grand Bal-Masque, to be given under the auspices of the 44th Regiment Dramatic Association, at the Barracks of Companies D and E,

On Monday Evening, February 23d, 1863.

FLOOR MANAGERS.

William Howard,	J. B. Rice, Jr.,	Harry T. Reed.
" D."	" E."	" E."

COMMITTEE OF ARRANGEMENTS.

Sergt. G. L. Tripp, Co. D.	Corpl. C. E. Tucker, Co. E.
" H. A. Homer, E.	H. Howard, D.
Corpl. Z. T. Haines, D.	J. H. Waterman, D.
" J. B. Gardner, D.	A. H. Bradish, E.
" J. W. Cartwright, E.	C. H. Demeritt, D.
" M. E. Boyd, D.	D. Howard, D.
F. A. Sayer, D.	E. L. Hill, A.

Tickets, Ten Cents, to be had only of the Managers.

Music by the New Berne Quadrille Band. Five pieces.

ORDER OF DANCES.

1.	March	Lee's Quickstep.
2.	Quadrille	Sullivan's Double Quick.
3.	Lancers	Richardson's March.
4.	Contra	Skittletop Galop.
5.	Redown	Odiorne's Choice.
6.	Quadrille	Surgeon's Call.
7.	Polka	Mary Lee's Delight.
8.	Contra	Stebbins' Reel.

INTERMISSION.

9.	Quadrille	Ham Fat Man.
10.	Waltz	Pas de Seul.
11.	Quadrille	Dismal Swamp.
12.	Contra	Friends at Home.
13.	Polka	"Long Acre."
14.	Quadrille	Dug-Out Race.
15.	Military Quadrille	Newell's March.

Generals Foster and Wessels, besides other officers of note, were there, and seemed to be much pleased. Some of the costumes were good. Deacon Foster (H. W. Johnson) walked about the barracks as natural as life. Patten, made up as a Howard-street Sport, was so good, that Capt. Richarson did not recognize him. Among others, Chum Ward showed to advantage as a lady, having borrowed a complete outfit for the occasion.

Promenading and flirting wound up the affair about eleven o'clock.

FEBRUARY 25.—A fine day, but a hard one for all. We were ordered out early, and marched across the city, over the long bridge, to the large plain, where we were reviewed by Gen. Foster. It was a splendid sight. About all that is left to Gen. Foster of the 18th Corps was on the field,—about 12,000 or 13,000 men, including cavalry and artillery, and was the largest body of men we ever saw together ; but it was tiresome to us who did the marching, and we were glad to be in the old quarters again.

FEBRUARY 28.—For the last two days we have had no drill out of doors, and very little guard. It has rained steadily. The "Dudley Buck" arrived yesterday with a large mail, and a lot of boxes have also made their appearance. We were mustered for two months' pay this forenoon, and in the afternoon, between the showers, began one of a series of base-ball games between men of the 23d and ours ; but the rain postponed it to the dim future. We find our barracks just the thing this weather, much better than tents, and thank our stars and the United States Government for them.

MARCH 3.—Rain, and nothing but rain ; only the cleanest companies relieved, and we caught it again, and some of us are checked as extra guard. And now for the first time our regiment is broken. Two companies, " F " and " B," going yesterday on picket at Batchelder's Creek, a few miles out of New Berne, towards Kinston. We have been idle now quite a while, and think it most time to be moved. Some say we are going as provost guard down town, but all we can do is to wait and take what comes. Frank Learned has been appointed corporal in place of Ramsey, who joined the band.

MARCH 5.—It has cleared up and is quite cold. We sent off a large mail this morning. Last night we came very near having our barracks destroyed. The funnel of one of the stoves dropped against the roof, igniting the boards, and as we had all turned in, it burned through the roof before it was discovered by a sentry. After burning a hole five feet square we mastered it, and turned in again.

MARCH 6.—To be noted. Our company was declared the *cleanest* company! Consequently no guard for us to-morrow.

Notwithstanding our *camp* is quite sickly, *we* have had no cases till now. Whitney was taken down suddenly while on guard on the night of the 4th. He was quite sick for a few days, but is now better, and we hope will be all right soon.

MARCH 8.—A little incident occurred yesterday, which is very gratifying to some of the boys, showing the confidence our captain places in their word, and what a narrow chance others of us had. Saturday is generally cleaning up day, and we understood there was to be no battalion drill. At noon Sergt. White notified us that there would be a drill at half-past one o'clock P.M. Three or four of us happened to be close to the cook-house door, and of course cleared out. Robbins was outside and out of hearing; we asked him to go with us, and he, being innocent of the order just promulgated, fell in. We put in no appearance till dress parade, but nothing was said till tattoo roll-call, when those who were absent were questioned. Robbins was the first victim, being nearer the right of the line than any of us. The question was, "Did you hear the order given by Sergt. White?"—"No, sir."—"Where were you?"—"Outside the building, sir." Which answers were satisfactory. When the captain came a little short of the centre of the company and found another victim, the brilliant idea struck the culprit to say, "I was with Robbins, sir." (So he was, afterwards.) Robbins corroborated this, and the captain, not happening to ask if the order was heard, *passed*; and one more was saved. It was a narrow escape, and perhaps the white part of the fib saved the guard-house a temporary boarder.

MARCH 13.—There has been nothing worthy of mention since the last date, excepting the heavy rain, till last night, when we had an opera, "Il Recruitio," which was excellently rendered. Gen. Foster and lady, and other officers and their ladies, attended; the two barracks of "F" and "B" being filled from top to floor.

MARCH 14.—We were expecting a gay time to-day, it being the first anniversary of the capture of New Berne. It was reported that besides a review we were to have various salutes and plenty of beer. We were awakened about five o'clock by a salute, and, although we growled at the early hour, started out to see the fun. We soon found the saluting was done with shotted guns. Belger and

Morrison were posted on the river bank, firing as fast as they could. The old " Hunchback," using her 100-pounder, and a little farther down stream, the " Delaware " pegging away at the woods beyond the little fort where the 92d N.Y. Regiment was stationed, they firing also and the river alive with shot and shell from the rebels. We were immediately ordered out in " light marching order," and it looked as if our breakfast as well as our beer would get stale.

Rumors were plenty. About ten o'clock it was reported that we were going across the river to relieve the troops there, but stayed quietly where we were, hearing everything and seeing very little. By four P.M. everything was quiet, and the company returned to barracks. A mail was distributed, and the boys are busy answering letters, for the boat leaves in the morning.

OFF FOR LITTLE WASHINGTON.

MARCH 15.— Sunday. Last night about supper-time, ten of Company E under command of Acting-Corpl. Emerson, were sent to Gen. Wessels as head-quarters guard, and after a severe night's duty in keeping the general's horses all right and his staff from straggling, were suddenly marched at " double quick " back to camp, to find the regiment packing and getting ready to start. We bade good-by to the old barrack after a hearty supper, and with flags furled and no music wended our way down town and aboard the steamer " Escort." Company E was stationed forward, and as it was dark we could see nothing, but found the soft places and turned in. We will miss Russell and his mule this trip, as he is on duty in New Berne and cannot leave. As we passed across Craven Street we saw him with his father, and bade them good-by, telling him to look out for what boxes might come. Not a very safe man, with his reputation as a *forager*, to leave our boxes with ; but it is the best we can do.

MARCH 16.—When we were called to breakfast at seven this morning we found we were steaming down the river and just entering the Sound, After a pleasant sail, we arrived at the wharf at Little Washington about four P.M., and marched with colors flying and band playing, by Grist's, to the earthworks, where we busied ourselves in an entirely new occupation,—pitching our shelter-tents for the first time. It was done finally, and after a fashion of our own ; and now we are trying to write, but are bothered, as the gas is poor.

MARCH 17.—This morning while eating breakfast we were ordered to " Strike tents." We supposed it meant march, but found it was for symmetry, and we pitched them again in a more regular manner ; having the privilege of messmates sleeping together, with the understanding that in case of being aroused in the night we will take our places in line with promptness *and snap*. After fixing up tents, several of us took a stroll down town, visiting the earthworks. The town is of little account ; the earthworks interest us more. They consist of a line of breastworks, extending from the river below to the river above the town, two miles or more in length. At the centre of the line is a star fort of ten guns, and at about equal distances on the line are four blockhouses with one gun each. At the Greenville Road is stationed an old 32-pounder called " Aunt Sally," cracked and battered, and held to its carriage by ox-chains. They told us this gun was the key to the fortifications.

MARCH 18.—Had a thunderstorm and gale this evening which nearly destroyed our camp, but the tents stood it as well as could be expected. We had a brigade dress-parade to-day, and had a good chance to see the troops stationed here. They consist of eight companies of the 27th M. V., two companies N. C. troops, one of cavalry, and one of artillery, with Col. Lee in command; in all about 1200 men. (Our colonel's report, 1863, to Adjt.-Gen. Schouler says the actual force was 1160 men). The parade was good, and after a dusty march, we found ourselves back in our tents again. We are wondering what we are sent here for. As yet we have seen no rebels, but watch the woods, supposing they are doing the same thing, waiting for us.

MARCH 19.—It has commenced to rain again, and we are in a fine condition, everything both in and outside the camp is in a damp state, with the wind continually lifting one end or other of the tent; but we eat our three meals after a fashion, and then turn in and sleep what we can, waiting for events.

MARCH 20.—One of the events came last night, or rather this morning at half-past four. " E " was ordered out and marched to the edge of the swamp, beyond Blockhouse No. 1, close to the river one side and the woods on the other, with water in front of us. It rained steadily, and we lay crouched against the wall of the building until it was too light for the rebels to surprise us; then we were faced about and marched to our tents. At noon we moved again. This time the change is for the better. We are down town in a deserted store. It was owned by a rebel; so we pulled down the counters and shelves, and soon had rousing fires. We don't know where the other companies are, but hope they have as good quarters as we are enjoying. We are told to expect an attack to-night, which expectancy is as common as "About this time look out for rain." Lieut. Newell told us to-day we might be in New Berne soon. A boat left to-day which took our mail. If it would only clear up, we had rather stay here than be at New Berne, as red tape, guard, &c., are of little account.

The captain delivered a tobacco ration to-day. The question is, " Did he buy or forage it?" We don't want him to get demoralized yet.

MARCH 21.—Rained all night; we were ordered out at half-past four this morning, and remained under arms till the pickets were changed. We are detailed for picket to-night, so about all we intend to do to-day is to sleep.

MARCH 22.—We had a regular old-fashioned rain last night for a change. At ten P.M., in the dark and storm, we started from town; marched about a mile and were posted around an old cart, a little way from the road. The company was divided, a squad taking the posts on each road, and two men sent to the rear on inside post. It was a hard night's duty, but came to an end at last, and at seven this morning we were relieved, and crawled back to town, finding our old store a palace.

MARCH 23.—A steamer came up this morning bringing a sutler. We made another move to-day, going back to our old place under the breastworks in our shelter-tents. Everything is wet through and uncomfortable; but we acknowledge we are handier in case of trouble. It is rumored we are going North to guard prisoners, and that Capt. Richardson, of " A," goes to New Berne to-day. Another rumor is, we are going to Plymouth to have another trial at Rainbow Bluff, but we had rather stay here. This morning our captain distributed towels, soap, plates, and knives and forks to each man. How or where he found them we don't know, but would have saved him the trouble of purchasing, if he had mentioned where they were. A mail arrived to-day.

MARCH 25.—Yesterday it rained most all day, and the drills Col. Lee had inaugurated Monday have not amounted to much as yet. We played cards, read, wrote letters, and slept; so the day worried out. To-day we have been firing at a target for a change. It was on a couple of bread-boxes, one on the top of the other, in the field immediately in front of our breastwork. The target was small,—only two feet square,—but still a few hit it.

MARCH 26.—No drills or excitement for two days, excepting a slight conflagration yesterday. Millar's tent caught fire and was destroyed; and last night many more were blown down by a high wind, with plenty of rain.

SIEGE AT WASHINGTON.

MARCH 30.—It has rained nearly all this week, and until yesterday we have been loafing, trying to kill time. Last night our company was on picket again up the road towards Tarboro, coming in this morning about six o'clock. They had a most miserable time. Twitchell was sent to the hospital sick. A few of us were on guard here, so escaped picket duty.

Gen. Foster arrived here this morning, and by noon Companies A and G, under command of Capt. J. M. Richardson of " A," with one howitzer, were tramping across the bridge towards New Berne on a scout. Those who could went to the water's edge to watch them. They were soon in action, meeting a force of rebels who handled them severely. Finding quite a strong force protected by breastworks, they were ordered back, to give the "Louisiana " a chance to shell the woods. Capt. Richardson of " A " was wounded twice in the left arm. They left Sergt. Hobart, Corp. Lawrence, and John Leonard of " G," who were taken prisoners. The rebels closed on them and carried them off. Several others were struck, but none seriously hurt. About every man at the head of the column was hit. Capt. Richardson was heard to say, " It is rough to go through what I have (five or six battles) without a scratch, and get hurt in this affair."

MARCH 31.—Last night about seven o'clock, as we were standing behind the breastworks looking towards the woods, we were startled by a flash, and heard a heavy report. The fort had opened fire upon the woods, the scene of our

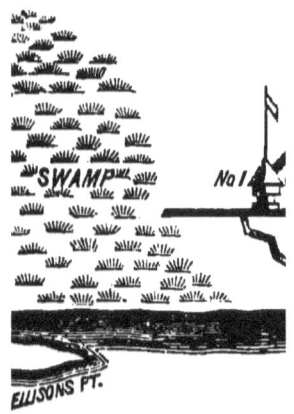

MAP OF WASHINGTON, TAR

picket duty. We were immediately under arms, and after a short march were halted at the edge of the town facing the fort. Here we stacked arms and waited. It rained all the evening, and the gun-boats kept up an incessant fire over our heads. We tried to sleep, but with little success. The house immediately behind us was full, so Robbins and myself crawled underneath for shelter. We awakened to find the regiment had moved. After diligent inquiry, and some walking, we found "E" in the Academy, where we passed the rest of the night. We left our quarters about noon, and moved to the breastworks at the left of the fort, where we heard that Gen. Hill had sent in a flag to the COLONEL IN COMMAND, demanding the surrender of the town. He must have been somewhat surprised to receive a reply from GEN. FOSTER, little thinking that he is here, and has no idea of giving up, at least on the first day.

Our breastwork is about five and one-half feet high inside, one foot thick on top, and from ten to twelve feet thick at the base, with a ditch outside. In front the wood is cut away for the distance of a mile. We pitched our shelter-tents close under the breastworks, leaving room to stand between them and the works, and things began to look home-like again. How long it will last remains for the rebels to say. We have built a house for our officers, by taking a roof from a shed in town, and making it water-proof, or hoping it will be so, and banking it up with dirt. Not a very handsome edifice, but better than none.

APRIL 1. — April fool's day ; but we have had no time to celebrate, for early in the day we were orderd to build a traverse. There has been cannonading all the afternoon between the gunboats and the battery down the river.

APRIL 2.—We worked all night on the traverse, which now looks like something; but it will take most of another day to finish it. Firing commenced about eight o'clock this morning, and has been continued at intervals all day. At four o'clock in the afternoon a detail of fifteen men from "E," with spades and guns, were sent across the river, towards the ground where "A" and "G" had their skirmish. Three of us were sent out on the road as picket, while the rest built a breastwork across the road, not far from the bridge. The country here is about all swamp. As we face up the road, on our right the river makes in close to us ; in front is a creek about twelve feet wide, and on our left the swamp — said to be impassable. Beyond the creek, about an eighth of a mile up the road, we could see the rebel picket quietly smoking a pipe ; so we did the same, but were soon disturbed by Gen. Potter, who came up and gave us orders not to expose ourselves to their sight, after which we lay down beside the road in the brush. We were relieved at dark by three men of "I," who said they were here yesterday, and heard from the rebel picket that the prisoners were doing well. Hobart was shot through the lungs, Leonard lost an eye, and Lawrence's wound was slight. The working party joined the company about seven o'clock.

APRIL 3. — Companies "I" and "E" are to alternate in furnishing what picket is needed across the river — about twenty men each day. Our party went over this noon. We had been up since three o'clock this morning, and manned the breastworks, but nothing came of it. The gunboats and Rodman's Point had a duel, lasting till nearly five o'clock. As we went over the bridge at noon we could see about two miles down the river, and all was peaceful—in looks. The outposts being placed, the rest of us spent our time pitching quoits with rings, which were found among the ruins of the old foundry (our camp), or crawled into the ovens and slept till six o'clock in the evening. Then we left camp : six on inside post, three on outside, and the balance at the breastwork. We do not like being away from the company, but day after to-morrow others will come over and we stay, changing work from picket to digging.

April 4.— Were relieved to-day about twelve o'clock by Company I, and moved to camp, where everything is as usual. The company have been hard at work on the trenches; and after resting a while, all turned out again, with spades as trumps, and at it we went. The "Ceres" run the blockade last night without being struck. The rebel batteries opened fire about dinner-time on Blockhouse No. 3. We were ordered to the breastworks, and the fort replied, making a fine noise for a little while.

April 5.—Sunday. There is very little doubt but that we are surrounded and besieged. We have come down to very small rations (small enough before) of pork and bread, and no beef ; and limited to half a dipper of coffee at a meal, while the work is increasing, and hard work, too. This afternoon two companies of the 27th went down the river to occupy a battery which the boats had silenced, but when they arrived there they found it not so silent, and came back with the loss of two men. Capt. Richardson made us a present to-day of some good tobacco, which came acceptable enough, as we were about out. This has been a quiet day till about four o'clock this afternoon, when the gunboats and rebel batteries at Rodman's Point commenced firing ; but we feel none of it up here.

April 6.—It is reported that Gen. Hill is a strong churchman, and will not fight on Sunday, which may be the reason we were not disturbed much yesterday. To-day we are still at work on our breastwork, sodding the top and leaving loopholes to fire through. We cut our sods from the fields on the edge of the town, conveying them to the works in carts and on poles with boards laid on them. It is a change from digging, so we *accept* it. Our cavalry vidette was fired on twice last night about ten o'clock.

April 8.—Yesterday, the outpost of the picket across the river, from our company, had an excitement of a new character. Our corporal (Cartwright), who was at the outpost, leaving his rifle, advanced up the road toward the rebel picket, waving a handkerchief. He was met by a squad of rebels under the command of a captain. Corpl. Jim gave himself up for Salisbury ; but with his accustomed nerve, was bound to face the music. He halted ; and the captain, halting his men, came forward, and the two sat on a log at the side of the road, talked over matters and things, and separated with mutual good feelings. Corpl. Cartwright heard from Hobart, who is not expected to live. Leonard and Lawrence will soon be well. After this affair was over (the officer of the guard coming up and finding the corporal gone), Cartwright had to make a personal call on Gen. Foster, who, after reprimanding him for holding communication with the enemy, against special orders (a fact of which Cartwright pleaded ignorance), he was allowed to return to the company, where he concluded to remain for the present.

A negro came in to-day reporting (so goes the story) that the enemy have 30,000 men and forty pieces of artillery, and propose attacking us to-night or to-morrow morning. They have kept up a heavy fire most of the forenoon on the gunboats and Blockhouse No. 4. If that force is outside, and they propose to come in, they probably won't be disappointed, as we have only a force of 1200 men, counting the negroes, besides the four gunboats, which carry about twenty-five guns all told, and we shall have to go to Salisbury if we do not have reinforce-ments soon. The Rodman Point battery has been firing most of the day, and a new battery has just been opened in the swamp nearly opposite where the "Louisiana" lies, but it was soon silenced. The boys at Blockhouse 4 are using the unexploded rebel shells.

April 9.—Aroused and ordered to the breastworks this morning at half-past three o'clock, and as usual nothing happened. "Our squad" is on picket for the next twenty-four hours, leaving camp at eight o'clock. The night relief turn in at the old foundry, and will have nothing to do but sleep till six o'clock in the evening. Some could not sleep. Tucker and Whitney left early, starting for a scout down the river, coming back late, wet and hungry, and having seen nothing. Allen and Pettingill started in another direction, and all they reported was the finding of a lot of cord-wood.

April 10.—We had a rough time last night, Patten and myself being the outpost victims. The water flooded the road knee-deep, wetting us through ; but we knew no one could crawl upon our post without being heard, on account of the splashing they must make. We were bothered only twice during the night : once when the corporal of the guard (Mason) waded to us, found we were awake, and retreated in good order ; and again as we sat on the old ammunition-box, soaked through, we were disturbed by something crawling over our feet. I struck at it with my gun, but made no impression. We supposed it was a moccasin. We were relieved about six o'clock this morning by Company I. Lieut. Johnson left us in charge of Sergt. Parsons, and we started for the breast-works. As we neared the fort, after leaving the town, we beheld a splendid sight, although it was an awkward position for us. The rebels seemingly have perfected their arrangements, for as we turned the brow of the hill they opened, and we had the pleasure of witnessing the first cannonade on this side of the town, and as we were directly behind the fort, we had a lively time in reach-ing the traverse. We could see the men beckoning, but did not know why. After repeated dodgings and rollings over, we reached the traverse, only to find it occupied by Company A, in command of Lieut. Coffin, who ordered us to "Move on !" We moved, although against our will, and at last found our own company, under a new traverse, nearer the fort. The boys had taken possession, and were making much sport at our mishaps in getting in. Millar's face was actually radiant; he was one of the lucky ones in getting in first. As he was corporal of the guard, we thought he should have stayed till the last, to see that we were all right, but he probably thought the last should be first in this affair. The company had had a hard time also, working nearly all night building the traverse with the bomb-proof behind it. Our tent was gone, and all our things scattered, but, after a deal of hunting, we found the remains, and proceeded to re-pitch. We worked all day enlarging our traverse and finishing our bomb-proof. The day all through was a hard one. Our captain must have felt flattered, it being his birthday; and I don't believe he had a chance to count or think of his age on account of the constant salutes from all directions. That is the reason, probably, why Sergt. Parsons hurried us in this morning, that he might be on hand to participate with Capt. Richardson in his celebration.

April 11.—Worked all night either on traverse or camp guard, or on " A's " traverse, " A " and "E" helping each other on both. Dr. Ware was buried to-day. He died yesterday of fever brought on by overwork. He was an excellent surgeon, and highly esteemed by both officers and men. Gen. Potter's orderly has been outside with a flag of truce ; but we hear no particulars. The flag-staff in the fort was struck several times to-day.

It is the rule to have a sentry at each end of the breastwork allotted to " E." Last night, the guard on the bomb-proof heard a noise about eleven o'clock, gave the alarm, and we were soon in line. We found the trouble arose from some outside picket, who got lost, and brought up against our breastworks. After some trouble, matters were arranged and we turned in again. What the man was doing so close in we have not discovered. Our traverse, being all done, will bear a slight description. Being on duty as picket the night it was built, I view it with different feelings from what the boys do who worked all night upon it, so can afford to write about it. It is at right angles with the breastworks, thrown up to a height of about fifteen feet. It is fully sixty feet long, about fifteen feet thick at the base, and six or seven feet at the top. We utilized the hole made by building this hill, by covering it with a strong roof, then covered that with sand a foot or two deep ; and as the Johnnies don't seem to use mortars, we feel tolerably safe, having a roof over our heads, in case of a sudden flight of meteors. Rumors to-day that reinforcements left New Berne last Wednesday, and we live in hopes that they will reach us.

April 12.—The rebels are getting a good range on our fort, and as we are in a direct line behind the fort from one of their batteries, we get what goes over them. We had been walking around outside the traverse,—even Gen. Foster was outside the fort, walking back and forth, probably thinking out the problem,—when about half-past nine o'clock we were brought to a realizing sense of our situation, for they opened on us " right smart," driving us all to the breastworks and bomb-proofs. One shell went through a tent, tearing up the ground where Sherman had just been sitting. The wooden shanty occupied by Sutton and Mann was demolished, and many others shaken up. We learn that the rebels have been reinforced both below and higher up the "Tar," which sounds bad for us. All this forenoon the gunboats have been pitching into the batteries at Rodman's. Another rumor is, that our extra clothes and ammunition are aboard a schooner below. We need both.

APRIL 13.—We heard pleasant music last night, it being heavy firing in the direction of New Berne. It must be our reinforcements, whom we heard had been turned back from Swift's Creek. The battery at "Widow Blunt's" shot away our flag-pole, yesterday, but it was immediately repaired. "E's" men were on picket across the river, last night, and had a lively time, the outposts consisting of Clough and Robbins. The rebels posted a gun to bear either on the gunboat or bridge, taking, in its course, our picket; and as soon as the "Louisiana" commenced shelling, the road was a sad place for a man who wanted to save his head. They got out of it all right, no one being hurt. One of the shots from the gunboat struck the old chimney, knocking bricks and mortar all over the reserve. Meanwhile the "Widow Blunt" batteries were raining shot and shell at the fort, making it lively for the homeguard.

APRIL 14.—Heavy firing last night down the river, and about midnight an immense amount of cheering. We were all called out, but found the cheering was on our side. THE "ESCORT" (*an unarmed steamer*), HAD RUN THE BLOCK-ADE AT RODMAN'S POINT, BRINGING UP THE 5TH RHODE ISLAND, COLONEL SISSON, which practically ends the siege, as we can probably send or bring vessels through the blockade any time. Robbins, Pierce, and myself have been detailed in the fort to-day, building a bomb-proof for Gen. Foster, but the fire from "Widow Blunt" was so lively we could do but little. We received a mail in the mêlée, bringing about $25 to our mess, being the first for several weeks— it seems to us months. I immediately left my watch with a jeweller in the 27th, who was in the fort, and who repaired it while under fire. I *now had the money* to pay him, thanks to home folks. We have been so hard up that a day or two since I tried for the first time to borrow a dollar or two, asking even Capt. Richardson. When he showed me that his pocket-book held only about two dollars, I gave it up. To-day I offered him some, when he showed me a bill which came by the same mail as ours. I think the full appreciation of the value of money will cling to us all, officers as well as men, in all future time. Our change of clothes came to-day, but in an awful condition.

APRIL 15.—"Our squad" on picket again across the river. As we were on the bridge this morning we saw the "Escort" steaming down the river, bound for New Berne, having Gen. Foster on board. We have had a pleasant day, but the water in the river is very high, consequently our camp and the road are flooded. When the dinner of boiled rice came, it took an extra amount of persuasion from the lieutenant of the guard, to make the man bring it to us, but he finally concluded to, and then had to carry it to the outpost.

APRIL 16.—When we arrived at the breastworks, this morning, we found "E" had been at work again. Strangers were at our old bomb-proof, and we had to hunt round some, but at last found the company had been assigned quarters in a good looking two-story house, close to Grist's mansion, owned by a Mr. Parmelee (probably no connection of the baker at the South End). Our things were in a decidedly second-hand condition ; in a pile under the front stairs. But we find our quarters so much better than those we had at the breastworks, that we do not complain. The house is badly shattered by shot and shell, one having traversed the building from corner to corner, tearing floors and plastering to pieces. To get these quarters we had to promise to be up, and at the breast-works in three minutes. We took the chances, and promised, of course.

While we were on picket last night we heard noises, which were unaccount-able, and reported them, on which a few shells were thrown into the swamp. At four o'clock this morning we heard the rebel drum beat for roll-call ; at five o'clock the bugle call for advance ; so we suppose the rebels have started. They came near to the creek, but it was so dark we could not make out much. We saw a man on a white horse at the picket post, as a lantern was in a position to throw a strong light on him. To-day Company I's picket advanced to the old earthworks, where Hobart, Leonard and Lawrence were taken, and found every-body gone from that side of the river. This forenoon, three companies, " C," " D " and " I " moved down the river to Hill's Point, which they are to occupy for the present. The following is the last order from Gen. Foster previous to his departure for New Berne : —

HEAD-QUARTERS, WASHINGTON, N. C., April 14th, 1863.

The commanding general annouces to the garrison of this town that he is about to leave for a brief time the gallant soldiers and sailors of the garrison.

Brig.-Gen. Potter will remain in command, and in him the commanding general has the most perfect confidence as a brave and able soldier.

The naval command remains unchanged ; therefore that arm of the defence will be as effective and efficient as heretofore. The commanding general leaves temporarily and for the purpose of putting himself at the head of a relieving force, and, having raised the siege, expects soon to return. But, before leaving, he must express to the soldiers under his com-mand, the 27th and 44th Mass. Vols., parts of the 5th New York Battery and 3d New York Cavalry, the 1st North Carolina Vols., his thanks for, and admiration of, their untiring zeal, noble emulation and excellent courage, which has distinguished them during the siege of this port ; and he feels confident that the display of those qualities under Gen. Potter will hold the place until the siege is raised.   (Signed)   JOHN G. FOSTER.

APRIL 17.—We had pleasant orders to-day, no more picket across the river ; only our breastwork guard, and only two at a time at that. This afternoon a party of us went to the river, by Grist's cotton store, and had a good swim, the first for a long time for some of us.

APRIL 18.—A jolly time last night; we tried to get up a good fire in our room and succeeded. We came very near setting the house in a blaze. After burning out the chimney and mantel-piece, we finally put it out, and the sergeant could not find out who did it. Another mail to-day, and on the same steamer, a part of the 43d. By our mail, we hear, some one wrote home that we had been in a severe all-day fight, and were badly whipped, having sixteen Cambridge boys killed and wounded. As there are only twenty-one Cambridge boys in the company, it would leave a small margin for our friends to hope on; and the chances of the Boston, Waltham and Watertown boys would have been small. Later news gave them a different version, although it was bad enough. We were enjoying ourselves last evening; even some of the sergeants were out on the river fishing for eels, when we heard a shot; a change came over us. The captain said we were at the breastworks inside of three minutes, where we lay down trying to get some sleep. Soon Sergt. Parsons came along the line, and picking out ten or eleven of the boys, started for Blackhouse No. 1, where we were joined by an equal number from Company B, 27th, and a negro volunteer. We cleared the breastworks, and pushed to the woods. After a diligent search for an hour, we were called in. We found that the cavalry picket had been fired on and wounded in the wrist. Coming in, two of us were invited to supper with the blockhouse boys. We accepted, of course, and as we were late in rejoining the company we got a scolding for not returning at once, but, considering the great temptation, we were let off easy. Capt. J. M. Richardson of "A" and our Lieut. Newell have started for New Berne. Lieut. Newell is not very well. Capt. Richardson of "A" is getting along fairly.

April 19.—One of the pleasantest days of the season; reminding us of the June Sundays at home. We have nothing to do, and very little to write about. This noon, while a party were on the roof of the house, we heard shouting down town, and soon saw troops crossing the bridge. Knowing it was Gen. Foster and the relief from New Berne, we tried to get away to see them, but the guard would not let us go, so we had to stay at home.

April 21.—We had a brigade dress parade yesterday afternoon, and to-day are cleaning up, preparing for embarking to-morrow.

HOME AGAIN.

April 22.—We started early this morning on the "George Collyer," bound for New Berne, having on board, besides our regiment, a part of the 46th Mass. Vols., and are towing a schooner with the three companies from Rodman's Point. We were having a fine sail, when the orderly picked up four of us, and now we are on guard below, away from all chance of seeing what is going on.

April 23.—We arrived at New Berne without special incident, about midnight. The regiment immediately left for the barracks; the lieutenant of the guard forgetting the poor guard on duty, so we, after one o'clock turned in, and had a good nap in the cabin, joining the company this forenoon, to find ourselves in the barracks formerly occupied by the 10th Connecticut. The barracks are not our own, and our boys are homesick; but we have found lots of boxes and have had a glorious lunch of what remained of our good things. They had been over-hauled, and there is a sad discrepancy between the list and the contents of the boxes.

APRIL 25.—Yesterday was spent in getting ready for, and to-day in taking possession of, New Berne, as Provost-Guard. It was done in fine style, all the colors flying, and white gloves on. There are three general divisions. No. 1 is at Provost Head-quarters, No. 2 is at the Atlantic Railroad office, and No. 3 is on Pollock Street. About sixty men at each division, making the duty quite heavy. Our captain being officer of the guard ; the first time that honor has been assigned to a captain. We lose one of our best men to-day, Charles E. Tucker. We are sorry to have him go ; but he will be the gainer. He takes a command in the 54th Mass. Vols. Several of the men from the regiment go home when he does. We wish them luck, and rapid promotion.

APRIL 26.—Our quarters are excellent. We have three houses on Broad Street, not far from the river ; two of them are two stories, and the other a cottage. The company is divided ; a part in each house, having its own sergeant; and each room has its own mess. We have only one set of cooks ; so we come together three times in the day for our rations. We don't like the arrangements on some accounts, but we are in the best quarters we have had since leaving Boston, so we ought not to grumble.

To-day we have been doing escort duty. Dr. Ware's body is to be sent North to his home, by the steamer " Terry." He died during the siege at Little Washington. He was a good man, and one of whom it may be truly said he " died at his post." Tucker goes home on the same vessel. Bowman is appointed corporal in Charlie's place.

APRIL 28.—Warm and rainy. Our guard is the same, however, rain or no rain. Most of our party are on the first district, distributed from the Gaston House door, round the wharves to the Provost Office. The posts are all easy enough, excepting those at the upper end of the town, near the camps. They are occasionally disturbed by runaways from the cavalry and artillery, who come down in the night without passes, and having no feeling for us, *try* to insist on passing where they have a mind; consequently a few get picked up, and stay down town all night.

Lieut. Cumston returned to duty to-day, having been away about four months, on detail with Brigade Ambulance Corps at Charleston ; and, of course, missing the nice cottage our officers had at Washington.

APRIL 30.—The weather is fine. Yesterday, we heard from the expedition, which left New Berne, lately, under Col. Jones, of the 58th Pennsylvania. They are near Kinston, only about four miles distant. They have had a skirmish, losing a few men. The " Escort " sailed North to-day. Our regiment was inspected this forenoon, at ten o'clock.

MAY 2.—Received to-day four months' pay, and consequently will have a good time. The flies are getting too thick for us ; we kill them off by scattering sugar and powder on the table. When the flies are thoroughly entertained with the sugar, we set the powder on fire, and the enemy succumb.

NEWBERNE, MAY, 1863.

MAY 4.—The "Dudley Buck" has arrived with a large mail for us, which, with the four months' pay we received on the 2d, makes us happy indeed. Fancy goods have to suffer now. Our quarters are full of store truck; but very little will keep over night, it is so hot.

MAY 15.—There is really nothing just now to write about It is getting terribly hot. We have our guard duty and drilling. There is a great sameness about the drill, but the guard duty gives us a change—one day here, the next at the other end of the town. A squad from our company, a day or two since, had to guard the small-pox hospital, not a very desirable locality ; but, as a compensation for that, on the other side of the street, close by, is the "Baltimore House," post 4. A short distance from the second district head-quarters is the graveyard, on which some of the boys dislike to stand, preferring the "hospital" or "Baltimore." The other posts in this district are good, especially the one close to the Neuse, where they report negro dances most every night. To offset these, we have the head-quarters of Gen. Foster, post 12, where we have to be on our taps all day.

In the 3d district, there are two hard posts, 5 and 6—the rest are easy. In the 1st district, there are no really bad ones, but some excellently lazy ones— being post 12, the bake-house, 9 and 20 the wharves, and 6 at the produce wharf.

Companies F and B have been home several days. They say they had a fine time building breastworks, and doing general picket duty.

MAY 26.—The expedition to Kinston resulted favorably for our side. They took a large lot of prisoners, who were sent to Fort Munroe to-day, Company F going as guard. Thermometer to-day only 102 in the shade.

MAY 27.—Yesterday we performed escort duty at the funeral of Col. Jones, 58th Pennsylvania Infantry. He was killed at Batchelder's Creek by a sharp-shooter. To-day General Foster has been advocating the idea of our re-enlisting in the new artillery regiment. Many probably will, but prefer going home first. Orderly White has left the company for a promotion, but will go home with us.

MAY 31.—Yesterday, on account of the discharge of Sergt. White, there were made four other changes, none of which struck our mess. Our second sergeant (Homer) has been appointed first sergeant, Corporal Allen is now fifth sergeant ; and Hight promoted to corporal. The petition came to Capt. Richardson, signed by all the men ; it shows how popular Harry has been—as a private ; and Fletcher is appointed lance corporal.

JUNE 2.—We received two months' pay to-day. The company is full, all details having reported this forenoon, and Company F returning a day or two since, our regiment looks more as it did at first.

JUNE 4.—We are getting ready to start for home; and shall probably move day after to-morrow, the 6th. But very little has been done to-day, except guard duty and dress parade, and preparing for a grand time Friday night. We have cleaned up the quarters, sold or boxed up our extra things to send home, and are waiting.

HOMEWARD BOUND.

June 6 —The boys fell into line this morning at seven o'clock, but being the last night in camp we did not get the usual amount of sleep, and this morning we look anything but up to our usual standard. We finally started, taking on the old guard, who were relieved the last thing by the 27th Mass. Vols. We marched in review before Gen. Foster, thence to the depot, escorted by the 3d Mass. Vols. We went on board a train of open cars (similar to the ones on which we came up, eight months ago), and started in a rain ; not as severe, however, as what we had at that time. About ten o'clock we arrived at Morehead City, embarked on the "Guide," bound for Boston and home. The companies aboard the "Guide" are "A," "G," "H," "K," and "E," with staff, band and sick, excepting a few, who were too ill to be moved, whom we left at New Berne ; the only one of our company being Ed. M. Pettengill, who was taken down while on guard, Friday, and had to be carried to the hospital. The "Geo. Peabody" takes the left wing, "F," "B," "D," "C," and "I," and left while we were at the wharf.

June 10.—After as pleasant a sail as could be desired by any one, we arrived in sight of Massachusetts, yesterday morning, steamed up the bay, arriving at Central Wharf about eight o'clock. A guard was immediately stationed across the wharf, to keep the boys from getting lost in the big city ! A few did get away, and run the risk. We were treated to a fine lunch, for which we were very grateful, by Messrs. Whall & Dyer, the fathers of Cliff. and George.

After the usual preliminaries of being received by the escort, consisting of the N. E. G. Reserve, Mass. Rifle Club, Battalion National Guards, and Roxbury Reserve Guard, we moved up State Street, which was crowded with our friends ; across the City to the Common, where, after some speaking by Mayor Lincoln, responded to by Col. Lee, we advanced upon our friends, and the tables at "double quick" for hand-shaking and lunch. We were then given a furlough till Monday, the 15th, when we were ordered to report at Readville, to receive our discharge. We started for the horse-cars (no more frogging for us), and by night most of us had had a good home wash, and a white shirt on for the first time for nine months.

June 16.—Reported at Readville at sunset last night, and are in the quarters occupied by the 45th Regiment last Fall. We find notices posted up, allowing us about six hours' drill a day. We thought we were over all that. We are to have regular guard, why, we cannot imagine, but are looking anxiously for the mustering officer.

June 18.—This diary has reached its limit. The company was disbanded to-day, with the rest of the regiment, and dismissed, probably forever. We have had our last drill, our last parade, our guns have been taken away, and we are a company only in remembrance of the time we were together. Now, each one is to take up his life, on his own individuality, and fight out his own fight for better or for worse.

READVILLE, JUNE, 1863.

ROSTER.

The * represents members of "Co. E Associates."

The number over the name corresponds with that of the gun
and the one in the group.

CAPTAIN,
* SPENCER WELLES RICHARDSON,
Richardson, Hill & Co.,
40 Water Street, Boston, Mass.

FIRST LIEUTENANT,
* JAMES SHUTTLEWORTH NEWELL,
St. Joseph, Mo.

Re-entered U. S. Service as first lieutenant, 5th Mass. Cav., December 29th, 1863 ; promoted captain February 15th, 1865 ; mustered out of service October 31st, 1865.

Was in action at Bailor's Farm, Petersburg, and Richmond, Va. From the surrender of Lee to time of muster out, was stationed in Texas.

SECOND LIEUTENANT,
* JAMES SCHOULER CUMSTON,
Hallett & Cumston,
1293 Washington Street, Boston, Mass.

Detailed as Chief of Ambulance Corps for General Stevenson's Brigade, to date from January 7th, 1863. Sp. Or. 75.

5
* GEORGE HENRY ADAMS,
Chester, New Hampshire.

2
* WILLIAM ROBERT ADAMS,
East Cambridge, Mass.
Detailed as carpenter November, 1862.
CORPORAL.

Re-entered the U. S. Service, August, 1864, in Co. H, 6th Mass. Vols., for three months' service. Doing guard duty at Arlington Heights, Va., relieving the old troops for General Grant, and guarding prisoners at Fort Delaware, on the Delaware River. Meeting some there who were against us at Little Washington in 1863. They said they were formed in line of battle three times to storm us, but did not know why it was not done.

1
WILLIAM ADAMS ALLEN,
Tillinghast, Allen & Co.,
Chicago, Ill.
Corporal until May 30th, 1863.
5th sergeant for remainder of service.

65
* FRANCIS BALDWIN,
496 Broadway, New York City.
Detailed as pioneer December 6th, 1862.

28
THEODORE LORING BARNES,
Discharged for disability April 3d, 1863, per order General Foster. Left New Berne April 5th. Sat up for the last time July 5th. Died April 5th, 1864. Buried April 8th, 1864, at Waltham, Mass.

82
* CHARLES HANAFORD BEDELL,
62 Worth Street, New York City.

52
EDWARD RICHMOND BLANCHARD,
413 Broadway, New York City.

13
* WILLIAM LAZELL BLANCHARD,
Stebbins, Grout & Co.,
90 Franklin Street, Boston, Mass.
CORPORAL.

29
* FRANK FOSTER BOWMAN,
Ellis Station, Norwood, Mass.
CORPORAL.

55
* ALBERT HENRY BRADISH,
179 5th Avenue, Chicago, Ill.
Re-entered the U. S. Service as Second Lieutenant 55th Mass. Vols., February 11th, 1864. Mustered out of service, June 27th, 1864.

41
JOHN BRYANT,
Charlestown, Mass.
CORPORAL.
Detailed for garrison duty, December 2d, 1862, at Brice's Creek.

91

EDWARD EATON BUTTERFIELD,

No. 2 Prospect Street, Boston, Mass.

February 13th, 1863, detailed as carpenter, to date from November 24th, 1862.

43

* JAMES WELD CARTWRIGHT.

22 Exchange Place, Boston.

CORPORAL.

Writes: That three weeks and a half after being mustered out of old Company E, 44th Regiment, I was mustered in the volunteer service again as Second Lieutenant in the 56th Mass. Vols. Infantry, and recruited my company from Boston, Worcester and New Bedford. On the organization of the regiment at Readville, Mass., I was commissioned First Lieutenant of Company C, Nov. 21st, and the regiment went to the seat of war, March 21st, 1864, and was assigned to the 9th Army Corps, Gen. A. E. Burnside commanding.

In May, we were ordered to the Army of the Potomac, and on May 5th, 6th and 7th, 1864, commenced our active campaign at the battle of the Wilderness. We were then in the following engagements : Spottsylvania 12th and 18th, North Anna River, Cold Harbor, Petersburg, Weldon Railroad, Mine Explosion, Poplar Spring Church, Hatchers Run, siege of Petersburg and capture. Incidental to the campaigning, I would say, that at the second battle of Spottsylvania Court House, May 18th, 1864, I had the honor to command my company, and the service then rendered caused my promotion to captain for 'coolness and bravery in battle.' (I quote this expression from the official announcement from the Adjutant-General's Office of this State, General Order No. 625, 1864.) I mention this fact because it not only reflects credit upon the officer, but honor upon the old comrades of Company E, and its gentlemanly officers, more particularly as I had associated with me in that engagement two comrades of Company E, 44th Regiment, my sergeants, Merril F. Plimpton and Edwin A. Wallace, who were afterwards made officers.

The date of my commission as captain was May 17th, 1864. Although there would naturally arise many incidents in a campaign of a very active nature, I will give you one more, because I was in command of my regiment at the time.

Our regiment started early on the morning of April 1st, 1865, for the final charge at Petersburg, Va., Capt. Z. Adams and Capt. Hollis, senior to myself in command. These officers were both left in the rear, during the capture of rebel battery 27, by our regiment, and that left me in command, after the occupation of the rebel line. It was during this period that the enemy made a determined effort to recapture the line we were on ; they succeeded in driving all our troops to the right and left, and I held our position with 150 men of the 56th Mass. Regiment, assisted by the 5th Mass. Battery. I quote the words of the Adjutant-General's Report No. 7, for 1866, published in December.

"On April 1st, 1865, the 56th Mass Regiment participated in the attack on Petersburg, Va. The regiment held for a long time the line of rebel works on the Jerusalem Plank Road, assisted only by the 5th Mass. Battery. All other troops were forced back and abandoned the line, and had not the 56th Regiment held the key point with great tenacity, the rebels would have regained the whole line."

We were relieved by the 61st Mass. Vols., and Duryea's Zouaves of New York, and won the day. This was the last engagement we were in. We were stationed at Burkeville Junction, guarding prisoners, the day Gen. Lee surrendered to Gen. Grant, and assisted in the parole of the Rebel army.

I am happy to say that I received only a slight wound during this campaign, being hit by pieces of a spent shell on left hand and on right shoulder, neither of which did me injury. As a matter of record, I would say that the only officer that assisted me at the Spottsylvania affair was a 44th Regiment comrade, Second Lieut. John D. Priest, than whom no more excellent officer was connected with our regiment ; he received the same distinction as myself, being promoted to First Lieutenant for gallantry.   He was killed in action, June 22d, 1864.

Our regiment was mustered out of service, July 12th, 1865, after participating in the grand review of the army at Washington, D. C., before the President

Yours,   JAMES W. CARTWRIGHT,

Late Corporal Co. E, 44th Mass. Vols., and Captain Co. C, 56th Mass. Vols.

77
* JONATHAN HOMER CHEENY,
Albany, New York.

32
* SAMUEL AUGUSTUS CLOUGH,
63 Chauncy Street, Boston, Mass.

30
HENRY CLAY CROSS,
Saugus Centre, Mass.

Detailed Jan. 2d, 1863, as hospital nurse, to date from December 22d, 1862, Special Order No. 64.

74
* GEORGE GILMAN CURRIER,
Canaan, New Hampshire.

WILLIAM DEAN,
Springfield, Illinois.
Discharged for disability at Boston, Sept. 30th, 1862.

97
* OLIVER CARPENTER DERBY,
1037 Washington Street, Boston, Mass.

Re-enlisted in the United States Service, November 20th, 1863, as Sergeant Company H, 3d Mass. Heavy Artillery. Mustered out of service, Sept. 18th, 1865.

23
* GEORGE LEIGHTON DYER,
111 Worcester Street, Boston, Mass.

Detailed December 2d, 1862, for garrison duty at Brice's Creek, Special Order No. 35.

8
* WARREN FRANK EMERSON,
Waltham, Mass.

46
* GEORGE EDWARD FILLEBROWN,
Arlington, Mass.
Detailed as pioneer, December 6th, 1862.

59

* JOHN PRESCOTT FLAGG, Jr.,
56 Franklin Street, Boston, Mass.
Mackintosh, Green & Co.
Left General Guide until we reached Little Washington, March, 1863.

67

* WILLIAM GRAY FLETCHER,
130 Tremont Street, Boston, Mass.
Appointed Lance Corporal, May 30th, 1863.

62

* JOHN FESSENDEN HAMMOND,
41 Worth Street, New York City.
Transferred from Company A, October 27th, 1862.

50

FRANK JENNINGS HASTINGS,
Wassaic, New York.
After our service in 1863 I obtained a position in the Commissary Department, under Capt. E. E. Shelton, of Boston, at New Orleans. From thence to Brownsville, Texas, as Post Commissary of Subsistence, where we remained until Gen. Herron evacuated the place. Thence to Baton Rouge, La., where I remained until the end of the war. After the war, I settled in New Orleans again, in the cotton buying business, with Gen. Herron. While there, I witnessed the riots of July 30th, 1866, and passed through the yellow fever epidemic of 1867, when upwards of 20,000 people were sick at once.
Now I am settled down in this quiet village in the flour, feed and grain business.

84

* WILLIAM THOMAS HAYES,
17 Tremont Row, Boston, Mass.

79

* HENRY ORMAND HIGHT,
10 Tremont Row, Boston, Mass.
Appointed Corporal, May 30th, 1863. Re-entered the United States Service as Second Lieutenant in the 82d U. S. C. T., November 12th, 1863. Promoted First Lieutenant, September 13th, 1864. Appointed Adjutant, November 25th, 1865. Promoted Captain, and assigned to Company A, June 4th, 1866. Made Major by Brevet, the 3d of April, 1867, to date from the thirteenth day of April, 1865, " For gallantry at the siege and assault on Fort Blakeley, in April, 1865." Mustered out of service, September 16th, 1866.

76

* SAMUEL AMBROSE HOLMES,
393 Federal Street, Boston, Mass.
Detailed as wagoner, December 1st, 1862, Special Order 32.

95

* HENRY AUGUSTUS HOMER,
Second Sergeant. Promoted First Sergeant, May 30th, 1863. Re-entered the United States Service, April 22d, 1865, as Captain 19th Mass. Vols. Infantry. Mustered out of service, June 30th, 1865. Died at Cambridge, December 11th, 1875.

33
* HENRY WALDO JOHNSON,
Agent McKee Rankin Troupe.

66
* PETER FANEUIL JONES,
40 Water Street, Boston, Mass.
Discharged for disability, March 9th, 1863.

37
* CHARLES FREDERICK JOY.

Re-entered the United States Service in August, 1863, as Sergeant, Company F, 2d Battalion, 2d Mass Heavy Artillery. Commissioned Second Lieutenant 54th Mass. Vols. Sept. 30th, 1864 ; First Lieutenant, March 30th, 1865 ; Captain, July 17th, 1865. Final muster out August 30th, 1865.

He writes : "My service in the Second Artillery was performed amid scenes familiar to the members of old Company E, as it was my fortune to be stationed at New Berne, N. C., in garrison at Fort Totten for several months, participating in the defence of New Berne at the time of its investment by Gen. Pickett, February, 1864.

April 29th, 1864, my company was ordered from Fort Totten to Fort Stevenson, situated on the Neuse River, some little distance to the front, from Camp Stevenson, the former home of the old 44th Regiment.

Here I rejoined the company June 1st, 1864, having been on duty at Fort Totten, as Post-Sergeant-Major, since November 14th, 1863. Nothing worthy of note transpired to relieve the dull, monotonous routine of garrison life during the remainder of my connection with the company, from which I was discharged, to accept commission in the 54th Regiment Mass. Infantry, which regiment I joined at Graham's Neck, S. C., sharing the varied experiences in the march to, and occupation of Charleston, garrison at Savannah, Ga., and subsequent service in South Carolina ; being for a large portion of the time on staff duty as Acting Assistant Adjutant General and Acting Aide-de-Camp.

I will close with mention of one expedition of two brigades under command of Gen. E. E. Potter (whom Company E will remember in North Carolina), from Georgetown, S. C., to Camden and return, in April, 1865, resulting in several engagements with the enemy, and the destruction of twenty-eight locomotives, one hundred and twenty-one cars, three bridges, one railroad machine shop, one new turn-table, a large quantity of trestle work and railroad material, three hundred and fifty-four bales of cotton, several mills, and a large quantity of corn.

In the engagement of Boykin's Mills, April 18th, we lost First Lieut. E. L. Stevens, a former member of Company E, who, while in command of the skirmish line, was shot through the head, and died at his post of duty, with his face to the foe."

21
AMORY HOLMAN KENDALL,
Waltham, Mass.

22
* FREDERICK AUGUSTUS KENT,
Naval Office, Custom House, Boston.

Re-entered the United States Service as Captain's Clerk, in the Navy. Was on the "Albany" flagship of North Atlantic Squadron, Admiral Hoff. Took the United States Commissioners to Samana Bay, when that place was leased to the United States. Afterward served on the United States flagship "Congress," Commodore Greene, on same station ; was in the Navy about four years.

94
BENJAMIN FLINT KING.

Re-entered the United States Service as First Lieutenant, Company B, 18th U. S. C. T., December 7th, 1863. In the following April was transferred to Company I, and the regiment and another consolidated, and designated the 80th U. S. C. T., May 1st, appointed Judge Advocate on General George L. Andrew's staff, and soon afterwards was detailed Provost Marshal. Returned to his regiment July 19th, 1864, serving with his company until his honorable discharge, August 10th, 1864. He died at Boston, January 24th, 1868.

49
* FRANK STRATTON LEARNED,
Post-office Box 1139, New York City.
Appointed Corporal, March, 1863.

27
* JOHN BEAVENS LEWIS, Jr.,
104 Pearl Street, Boston, Mass., and Shreveport, Louisiana.
Administrator (Alderman) of Shreveport for the years 1866-1867.

85
WILLIAM BELDEN LIVERMORE,
Died in Charlestown, September 23d, 1870.

80
* THOMAS LOHEED,
368 Washington Street, Boston, Mass.

88
ABNER BICKNELL LORING, Jr.,
Died at Boston, March 25th, 1872.

87
* JAMES WARREN LOVEJOY,
614 North 4th Street, Camden, New Jersey.
Detailed as carpenter, February 13th, 1863, to date from November 24th, 1862.

86
FRANKLIN DEXTER MAGOUN,
East Cambridge, Mass.

60
ISAAC GARDNER MANN,
Mann & Beals.
91 Huron Street, Milwaukee, Wisconsin.

10
THOMAS DOWS MASON,
291 Broadway, New York City.
Corporal.

69
* ANTHONY FRENCH MERRILL,
Milwaukee, Wisconsin.

40
* LESLIE MILLAR,
34 West Street, Boston, Mass.
CORPORAL.

3
EDGAR VICOUNT MOORE,
83 1st Avenue, New York City.

92
* JOHN FREDERIC MOORE,
Waltham, Mass.
Fifth Sergeant until November 2d, 1862 ; Fourth Sergeant until May 30th, 1863; Third Sergeant for remainder of service. Acted as commissary and company clerk.

64
* ALFRED LOWELL MORSE,
22 and 24 White Street, New York.

81
CHARLES MORSE,
Killed in action at Rawle's Mill, North Carolina, November 2d, 1862.

JOHN HENRY MYERS, Jr.,
DRUMMER.
Re-entered United States Service as Sergeant in Squadron H, 3d Battalion, 4th Mass. Cavalry, February 8th, 1864. The Battalion was at Hilton Head until May 12th. Thence to Newport News, and then was transferred to the department of Virginia and North Carolina. Engaged on picket duty till June 16th, 1864. Then "H" was ordered on scouting duty and courier service. August 16th, the whole command reported to Gen. Birney, 10th Army Corps ; August 24th, occupied position in front of Petersburg. When the Army of the James moved from winter quarters in March, 1865, "H" remained with the 25th Corps before Richmond, and were the first troops to enter the city, April 3d. The guidons of "H" and "D" *being the first Union colors carried into Richmond*, and raised by Union troops. Was mustered out of service with his regiment, November 26th, 1865.
Died at Chelsea, January 21st, 1873.

25
ALBERT KIDDER PAGE,
Died at Boston, July 3d, 1863.

26
CHARLES STUART PARK,
Savannah, Georgia.
Writes : In August, 1863, I was commissioned Second Lieutenant in the 56th Regiment Mass. Vols., but was not mustered into service, as I wished to enter the Navy. In October, 1864, was commissioned as Acting Assistant Paymaster in the Navy, and was, in November,

attache1 to the United States steamer "Chimo" (a torpedo boat, 4th class), Acting Master John Dutch commanding. In January, 1865, proceeded to Brooklyn Navy Yard, thence in April, to Hampton Roads and Washington Navy Yard; was detached in June, 1865, ordered to Washington to settle accounts, and was honorably discharged in August, 1865, receiving certificate and thanks of department on final adjustment of my accounts in January, 1866. We were engaged in no fights; the only smart thing we ever did, was as a guard by sea on a camp of rebel prisoners, about 20,000, on the day succeeding the night of President Lincoln's assassination, being the only gun-boat there for twenty-four hours—an uprising of the camp being momentarily expected.

12
MICHAEL ALLEN PARSONS,
Company L, 5th United States Cavalry, Fort McPherson, Nebraska.

Promoted Fifth Sergeant November 2d, 1862, for bravery, at Rawle's Mill, N. C.; Fourth Sergeant from May 30th, 1863.

He writes, under date of March, 1878 : Your letter came this morning, and in reply 1 would say, that I enlisted in New York on the 22d of February, 1873, in Company L, 5th United States Cavalry; made a Corporal in 1874; promoted Sergeant in 1875; and re-enlisted February 22d, 1878, in the same company.

I am first on the list of non-commissioned officers to be recommended for a commission, if the new bill passes Congress.

Since I have been here, I have been all over Arizona, and fought in nearly all the engagements with the Apaches, under Gen. Crooke. When he came to this department, he applied for, and got this regiment We have scouted for the last two years in the Black Hills country, and had a great many skirmishes and battles with the Sioux, Arrapahoes and Cheyennes. Our company has been twice to the Custer massacre ground,—once with Gen. Sheridan, when we escorted him all through the Big Horn Mountains, and once when we followed a large body of Sioux north, to Powder River, where we had a fight for two days, and finally captured and killed all of Dull Knife and Crazy Horse's band, 900 ponies, and destroyed all their provisions. This was in November, 1876. We have had a running fight with Sitting Bull for a month at a time, but never could make much out of it, as he was too strong. I cannot recollect all of what would interest you, but I remember all our good times in old Company E. This is a very exciting kind of life, and very healthy. Give my regards to all the fellows you see. Your friend and old comrade,

M. A. PARSONS.

35
* THOMAS HENRY PATTEN,
Denver, Colorado.

Re-entered the United States Service December 11th, 1863, as Sergeant, Company I, 2d Mass. Heavy Artillery ; promoted to Second Lieutenant Jan. 17th, 1865. Mustered out of service Sept. 3d, 1875. Was at second battle of Kinston, and did provost duty there after the surrender of Gen. Johnson to Gen. Sherman ; commissioned Second Lieutenant 54th Mass. Vols. February 22d, 1865, but was never mustered.

9
* JOHN HODGES PEARCE,
45 Lispenard Street, New York City.

63
* HENRY THOMPSON PEIRCE,
Physician, 247 East 116th Street, New York City.

53
* EDWIN MONTAGUE PETTINGILL,
53 Broad Street, Boston, Mass.

54
GEORGE FREDERICK PIPER,
48 Congress Street, Boston, Mass.

Writes : After being mustered out of service at Readville (not re-enlisting), I entered Harvard College, graduating in 1867. Then entered Harvard Law School, and finally commenced practice in 1869. Was elected member of the Common Council of the City of Cambridge for the years 1873-'74 and '75, being President of the Council during 1874 and 1875. Elected Alderman for the City of Cambridge for the years 1876 and 1877, and am now practising law at 48 Congress Street, Boston.

17
MERRILL FRANCIS PLIMPTON,
Fitchburg, Mass.

Writes : Re-entered the service Feb. 20th, 1864, as Sergeant, Company C, 56th Mass. Vols.; commissioned Second Lieutenant, July 1st, 1865 ; mustered out July 12th, 1865, by Special Order 162, Head-quarters Department Washington, D. C. Was in all the battles of Grant's campaign in Virginia,—Wilderness, Spottsylvania, Cold Harbor, North Anna River, all the battles in front of Petersburg, including the Mine Explosion, where I was wounded by a shell in the thigh, and by rifle ball in the hand ; was also in the battle when Petersburg was taken, the 56th being one of the first to enter the City ; was also in the immediate vicinity when Lee surrendered.

31
BENJAMIN FRANKLIN POND.
In 1864 lived at Belmont, Mass.; since then residence unknown.

68
GEORGE BARKER POPE,
Waltham, Mass.

90
* FITZ JAMES PRICE,
400 Washington Street, Boston, Mass.

* GEORGE LINCOLN PULSIFER,
Dartmouth Street, Boston, Mass.
DRUMMER.

58
* EDWIN AUGUSTUS RAMSAY,
Holyoke, Mass.
CORPORAL.
Entered Band, March 1st, 1863.

6
SAMUEL GREENLEAF RAWSON.
Died at Boston, March 5th, 1865.

83
* HARRISON TYLER REED,
1 Hancock Street, Boston, Mass.

19
* JAMES BAYARD RICE, Jr.,
Dyer, Taylor & Co.,
36 Chauncy Street, Boston, Mass.
COLOR CORPORAL.

57
* EDWARD RICHARDSON,
Physician, Westminster Hotel, New York City. Taken sick on steamer "Merrimac," October 24th, 1862. Discharged from Academy Green Hospital, January 12th, 1863. Received twenty days' furlough, February 28th, came to Boston and was discharged from the service, March 24th, 1863.

16
* JAMES ARTHUR ROBBINS,
Re-entered United States service, February 18th, 1864, Company E, 57th Mass. Vols. promoted to Q. M. Sergeant. Was in the following battles: Wilderness, Spottsylvania, North Anna, Cold Harbor, Petersburg, Weldon Road, Popular Spring Church and Hatchers Run. March 25th, 1865, the regiment captured the flag of the 57th North Carolina Infantry. Mustered out of service with regiment, July 30th, 1865.

42
* CHARLES HENRY ROBERTS,
Second National Bank, New York City.
Wounded in left arm, near shoulder, November 2d, 1862, at Rawle's Mill, near Williamston, N. C. January 8th, 1863, detailed as nurse in Hospital. January 14th detailed to report to Lieut. Goldthwaite, A. C. S. Discharged March, 1863 on account of disability.

11
* GEORGE RUSSELL,
41 Commercial Wharf, Boston, Mass.
Detailed in February, 1863, as superintendent of wood to report to Capt. Straight. Returned to Company, April 25th, 1863.

WILLIAM SAWYER,
Residence unknown.
Discharged for disability, Sept. 30th, 1862.

71
WALDO BLANEY SAMPSON,
35 Spring Street, Boston, Mass.

73
JOHN MURRAY SHERMAN,
Waltham, Mass.

4
* EDWARD PEREZ SMITH,
Waltham, Mass.

7
GRANVILLE SMITH,
Died in Virginia, October 27th, 1873.

14
EDWARD LEWIS STEVENS.

Re-entered the United States service as Second Lieutenant, Dec. 16th, 1864. Promoted First Lieutenant, Dec. 16th, 1864. Killed in action at Boykin's Mills, near Camden, S. C., April 18th, 1865, about a week after Gen. Lee surrendered. It is supposed he was the last man killed in the war; if so, Massachusetts gave the first and last offering to the rebellion. Ned was in Harvard College at the close of his Junior year, when "E" was recruited, but returned in 1863 ; as he wrote to his class secretary "Just in time to be present at Cambridge on Class Day. During the autumn of 1863, I studied and made up the studies of Senior year, passing my examination the last of October. I received my degree, January, 1864.

On November 12th, 1863, I commenced business in the store of Messrs. Sabin & Page, Boston, where I continued until March 15th, 1864. I then left in consequence of being commissioned in the 54th Mass. Vols. I leave Massachusetts to join my regiment now stationed in Florida, in a few days. My plans for the future are very unsettled. I shall probably remain in the army if life and health are spared me until the war is over. Heaven only knows what is before me; whatever it may be, I hope never to disgrace the class to which I am proud to belong, or the State which sends me to fight for the nation's life and freedom."

The career of Lieut. Stevens after he joined the 54th Mass. Vols. is identical with the regiment. He was killed at the battle of Boykin's Mill, April 18th, 1865, during an expedition to Camden, under Brigadier-General Potter, which left Georgetown, April 5th, 1865. The following obituary was drawn up by his comrades, among whom were Tucker, Joy and Whitney of old "E."

"He fell so near the enemy's works, that it was not deemed right to *order* any one forward to receive the body; but men promptly presented themselves, on a call for volunteers for that duty. The body was recovered and buried near where he fell. Lieut. Stevens' death carried a more than ordinary sense of grief among his brother officers. He was respected and beloved by every one in the regiment. His simplicity and frankness of disposition, his social and generous temper, combined with strong principles and an earnest devotion to what he believed just and right, made up an unusually pure and noble character. With perfect simplicity and modesty, he united firm convictions, and an unhesitating openness in avowing them. As an officer, he was efficient and faithful in the performance of his duties in camp, and fearless and daring in action; and though he disliked the military profession, and longed for peace and a return home, he had no thought of leaving the service until the success of the cause was decided. His comrades lament the loss of a brave soldier and a true friend and gentleman." [Vol. 2. Harvard Memorial Biographies.]

44
CHARLES CUNNINGHAM SUTTON,
Died at Boston, March 31st, 1869.

20
JOHN TACKNEY,
500 Washington Street, Boston, Mass.

93
* ALBERT FRANCIS THAYER,
Maple Hill, Kansas.
Third Sergeant until May 30th, 1863; Second Sergeant for remainder of service.

15

* HERMON CHANDLER TOWER,
Hudson, Mass.

Detailed as pioneer, in place of Baldwin.

78

* SAMUEL PAYSON TROTT,
59 Clarence Street, Boston, Mass.

Detailed as wagoner, December 1st, 1862. Special Order 32.

51

* CHARLES EDWARD TUCKER,
Portland, Maine.

Corporal November 2d, 1862. Discharged by order of Gen. Foster, April 26th, 1863, to take commission in the 54th Mass. Vols. Second Lieutenant, May 13th, 1863; Captain, February 3d, 1864. Final muster-out, August 20th, 1865.

He writes: Upon being discharged from Company E, at New Berne, N. C., to accept commission in the 54th Regiment, I immediately proceeded North, and joined that regiment at Readville, Mass., remaining with it during its entire term of service in South Carolina, Georgia and Florida, never being absent on leave or for sickness, and participating in all the battles and skirmishes in which the regiment was engaged, among which are Fort Wagner, Siege of Charleston, Olustee, James Island, Honey Hill, and Boykin's Mills.

In the assault upon Wagner, July 18th, 1863, I was wounded by a bullet from the fort going through my hat and cutting my head, notwithstanding which, I remained with the regiment, and when repulsed, I rallied about twenty men, under cover of a small sand hill, and waited to join a second charge, which was not made, however, and I retired with the men to within the picket lines. *We were the last men that came in from the assault.*

The most exciting incident in my soldier life, and one which tried my nerve more than any other, occurred during the night of the 11th of April, 1865. On that day the regiment had been detached from the main column at Manchester, S. C., and ordered to Wateree Junction, to destroy railroad material, which we did very effectually, besides capturing a train of cars. Steam being up in the engine, and the train ready for use, we concluded to avail ourselves of the opportunity of saving a hard march, and of taking the quickest method of rejoining the main body of troops. The men were speedily embarked, and I took the post of engineer, and after proceeding a few miles we came in sight of a stretch of trestle-work bridge which was on fire. Knowing that any delay would be dangerous, and that life or death hung in the balance, I crowded on all steam, and we crossed the bridge through flame and smoke in safety, but with not a moment to spare; for scarcely had we accomplished its passage when it tottered and fell a heap of blazing ruins. We rejoined the column at Singleton's plantation, on the Statesburg road, at eleven o'clock in the forenoon of the 12th.

A week from this time, Lieut. E. L. Stevens, a member of old Company E, was killed in action at Boykin's Mills on the 18th, and his loss was deeply felt by the whole regiment, as he had endeared himself to all, by his kind and genial disposition, courteous deportment, and soldierly bearing.

During the time of performing garrison duty at Charleston, I was detailed as Provost Marshal, acting in that capacity until the muster-out of the regiment in August, 1865.

18

CHARLES TYLER,
Detailed as cook.

Died at East Cambridge, February 21st, 1871.

36
NATHAN R. TWITCHELL,
Fremont, Kansas.

48
* GULIAN HENRY VAN VOORHIS,
Everett, Mass.

24
* GEORGE PHINNEY WALCOTT,
66 Chauncy Street, Boston, Mass.

Re-entered the United States service Sergeant Company F, 5th Mass. Vols., August, 1864, stationed at Fort McHenry, Maryland, on general guard duty. Mustered out of service, November 20th, 1864.

70
EDWIN A. WALLACE,
Residence unknown.

His subsequent military career has been kindly furnished by his Captain (Cartwright). He re-enlisted in the autumn of 1863, in Company C, 56th Mass. Vols., was made Sergeant, and went with his company to the front, commencing active service at the battle of the Wilderness. He participated in the battles of Spottsylvania and North Anna River, at the latter place coming out of the engagement safely, but missing his comrade, Sergt.-Major Crowley, he went in search of him, but was surrounded by the rebels. He was carried to Richmond, and thence to other prison pens, including that black hole of the Rebellion—Andersonville, Ga. He was exchanged at Millen, Ga., and joined our regiment before Petersburg, Va. He was promoted to First Lieutenant, and commissioned October 22d, 1864. The only engagements he participated in were reconnoissance to Hatchers Run, and the final attack at Petersburg, Va., where he behaved admirably, and reflected credit on himself and old Company E. He was mustered out of service honorably July 12th, 1865.

45
* WILLIAM FLAGG WARD,
Cambridgeport, Mass.

JOSHUA BREWSTER WARREN,
Boston, Mass.

Discharged Sept. 30th, 1862, for disability. Served afterward under Gen. Cook, in the West.

38
* CLIFTON HOWARD WHALL,
52 High Street, Boston, Mass.
Whall, Macomber & Tolman.

* GEORGE WILLIAM WHEELWRIGHT, JR.,
SERGEANT.

Discharged Sept. 30th, 1862. Went to the Army of the Potomac as Assistant Sanitary Agent, for the city of Roxbury, and served in that capacity about three months, until obliged to give up on account of sickness. February 9th, 1863, the Roxbury City Government passed a vote of thanks for that service.

Early in January, 1863, I went with Mr. Gibbs in charge of schooner "W. H. Frye" to New Berne, rejoined the 44th as volunteer and acted as Colonel's Orderly on the Plymouth or "Ham Fat" expedition. The day after the grand review, February 26th, 1863, was taken down with pneumonia, was sent to "Stanley" General Hospital, March 6th, and by March 16th was convalescent so as to be able to go North. This closed my army experience.

96
* EDWARD PETERS WHITE,
C6 Fulton Street, New York City.

FIRST SERGEANT.

Discharged May 30th, 1863. Re-entered United States Service, June 4th, 1863, as Second Lieutenant 2d Mass. Heavy Artillery ; promoted First Lieutenant, August 14th, 1863. Discharged Jan. 7th, 1865, honorably.

56
WILLIAM LAMBERT WHITNEY, Jr.,
Council Bluff, Iowa.

Re-entered the United States Service as Second Lieutenant 54th Mass. Vols. December 4th, 1864. Promoted to First Lieutenant, June 1865. Was acting Adjutant about three months. Mustered out August 20th, 1865.

He writes: I was anxious to join my regiment as soon as possible after receiving news of my appointment. Sailed from New York in the "Arago," in company with nine hundred bounty jumpers, deserters, &c., who were on their way to join Sherman's army. There was plenty of liquor among them, which increased the trouble. On the second morning I was detailed as officer of the day, and succeeding in finding the source of supply of the liquor in the fire-room, which supply being stopped, we finally restored order.

On reaching Hilton Head, I found the "Nelly Baker" (well-known in Boston Harbor), just ready to leave for Beaufort ; there I could learn nothing of the 54th, except that it was "up country," and learning from a quartermaster that the regiment was farther up on the other side, started in the steady rain in a boat he loaned me. It was as dark as any night I ever saw when we reached the landing (a broken-down dock) ; when I had landed and the boat had dropped down stream, I was alone in a strange country and in utter darkness. I managed to get off the dock and made my way to a shanty ; here I found two men who gave me very indefinite directions as to where the 54th was. I struck out across a marsh, and about every fifteen feet would bring up and feel round to find where the road, or more properly, the track had gone to. I then tackled a corduroy, which was varied by road with no corduroy, and in fact with no road. But after a while I reached camp and found Capt. Tucker and Lieuts. Stevens and Joy, and other old 44th boys, who gave me a warm reception. There being no vacancy, I waited some time for an assignment, but upon the vacancy caused by the death of Lieut. Webster, I went to Hilton Head, leaving Pocotaligo Station the same time the regiment did. After getting my papers, and being mustered in at Hilton Head, I reached the regiment again after a long and hard tramp. I was in hopes of being placed in Charley Tucker's company, but was assigned to Company G, placed on picket on Sherman's extreme right and front, and moving towards Charleston, which place we reached in February, 1865. After being on the outskirts of Charleston a while, we were sent to Savannah, Ga., where I was soon detailed to act as Adjutant. We did not stay there long, but went to Georgetown, S. C. From there we made a raid into the State, as far as Camden. We had considerable skirmishing, and on the 18th of April lost Ed. Stevens, who was shot in the head. At Wateree Junction we captured a train of cars all ready to move, but came on the rebels so suddenly that they jumped out and ran. Lieut. Swails was wounded in the arm, and I rode on one of the engines to help him run it. There were five engines on the train, but only two had steam up. Capt. Tucker took charge of the other train. On our way back, we received notice, through flag of truce, of the cessation of hostilities, and reached Georgetown without opposition. Then we went to Charleston, and were quartered in the

Citadel. In the meantime I had been promoted to First Lieutenant, and assigned to Company K ; and as there was no Second Lieutenant, and the Captain was acting as Provost Judge, I was in command. Was ordered to Fort Johnson, James Island, to dismount guns. Was relieved in July, and went to Mt. Pleasant. At that time I was ordered to take command of Company A, and " A " being entitled to the right of the line, I had the honor of marching at the head of the column, "up State Street," on the day of its reception.

89
* VICTOR AUDUBON WILDER,
165 Broadway, New York City.

47
* WILLIAM SULLIVAN WILDER,
9 Norton Place, Cambridge, Mass.

61
JAMES CUSHING WORTHLEY,
Hallowell, Maine.

He writes: I re-enlisted July 7th, 1863, as private in the 12th Unattached Company Heavy Art'y. When the 3d Regiment Heavy Artillery was organized, was appointed Commissary Sergeant, and June 25th, 1865, promoted to Second Lieutenant. Discharged the 29th of September, 1865.

34
* JOHN JASPER WYETH,
31 State Street, Boston, Mass.

APPENDIX.

Scarcely had we been dismissed from the United States Service, when our services were demanded again to help suppress the draft riots in Boston.

The regiment was ordered out on the 14th of July, 1863. " E " turned out 57 men. Part were sent to Chickering's Factory, another squad to each, the West Boston, Federal and Dover Street bridges, at the corner of Dover and Washington Streets, and at the Provost Marshal's in Sudbury Street, serving seven days, and being dismissed on the 21st of July.

FAREWELL SUPPER.

AUGUST 3d, 1863.—The members of " E " met at Parker's, and partook of our farewell supper. Nearly all were present, and had an enjoyable time. At this supper a committee was chosen, consisting of Capt. Richardson, Lieut. Newell, Sergt. Thayer and H. T. Reed, to hold and expend the balance of the Company Fund as might be needed by the men. The following is the " Company Song," by Harry T. Reed, to the air of Old Lang Syne : —

Hail, joyous hearts! let hand and voice
Proclaim us ONE to-night,
And Union, ever be our choice,
A Union true and bright.
Loud let our merry laugh peal out.
Let happy thoughts resound,
Our mothers know that we are out.
And Provosts are not round.

No more we cool our aching feet
In Carolina's soil,
No more we drill, advance, retreat,
In danger, blood, or toil.
Fill high, sing loud, join hands, my boys,
For on our festal day,
In happy thoughts, 'mid present joys,
We'll drive dull care away.

The sharp reveillé calls not here
The watchworn from his rest,
To-night we'll drink to mem'ry dear;
Love crowns our banner crest.
Then let our merry laugh ring out,
Let happy thoughts resound.
Our mothers know that we are out,
And Provosts are not round.

Now, comrades brave, the sacred past,
Our future's shadow be,
In happiness we end at last
This soldiers' company.
Then sing the chorus loud and strong,
Let heart and voice re-shout,
For we are doing nothing wrong,
And *taps* are just played out.

Whatever fates our footsteps sway,
As years their laurels twine,
We'll not forget this parting day,
For Auld Lang Syne.
For Auld Lang Syne, my boys.
For Auld Lang Syne,
We'll have a cup of kindness e'er,
For Auld Lang Syne.

RETURN OF OUR FLAGS.

On the 22d of December (Forefathers' Day), 1865, we met at Boylston Hall, and with the other companies proceeded to the Common. The procession started about eleven o'clock, headed by the escort, consisting of the Independent Corps of Cadets. The route was from the Common to Tremont Street, to Hanover, to Blackstone, to Clinton, to Commercial, to State, to Washington, to Essex, to Harrison Avenue, to Dover, to Washington, to Union Park, to Tremont, to Pleasant, to Boylston, to Arlington, to Beacon, to the Common; upon reaching the Common the colors were carried to the State House, and placed in care of the State, and we dismissed.

"COMPANY E ASSOCIATES."

In the latter part of January, 1872, circulars were sent to all members of the old company, whose addresses could be obtained, for a camp-fire, to be held at John A. Andrew Hall, Boston, on the 6th of February, which was attended by twenty-five men.

We formed an association with the above name. The object of this association is: First, to renew friendships formed during our service; Second, to raise a fund by which any needy members of " E " might be assisted.

We have held annual re-unions each year since, on the second Thursday of each December, and propose to do so as long as we can muster a man. (One of our company stopped me on the street lately, and asked when the next meeting would come off; our last was his first, as he had been out of the State for ten years. He regretted having missed so many, and wished we could have them every six months till he could catch up). Our first president was Capt. Richardson, who was re-chosen in '73. Then George Russell in '74, '75 and '76, he refusing to be a third termist. At our last annual meeting the following officers were chosen for the succeeding year : —

President, ... JAMES B. RICE, JR.
Vice-President, ... JAMES W. CARTWRIGHT.
" . . . . . . GULIAN H. VAN VOORHIS.
Secretary, ... JOHN J. WYETH.
Treasurer, ... CLIFTON H. WHALL.

The Treasurer reported at this meeting the amount of cash on hand to be $226.64. Which includes the balance of Company E Fund held by Capt. Richardson, and was turned over to us in 1874. This amount has since been increased by about $36. Below is the detailed account of our Company Fund from its inception to the $23 passed to the Association, which has been kindly furnished by Capt. Richardson for your perusal : —

RECEIPTS.

Donation Hon. Horace Gray	$100.00	
" J Murray Howe	100.00	
" Franklin King	25.00	
" Horatio Harris	20.00	
" William Cumston	500.00	
" F. Skinner & Co.	100.00	
" Gorham Rogers	10.00	
" Through C. H. Roberts	100.00	
		$955.00
City of Boston Account Recruiting Expenses		96.00
Company Savings September, 1862	$ 71.44	
" October, "	105.50	
" November, "	82.25	
" December, "	79.45	
" January, 1863	68.14	
" February, "	148.06	
" March, "	144.68	
" April, "	159.80	
" May, "	159.35	
		1018.67
		$2069.67

PAYMENTS.

Recruiting Expenses, Band, Posters, Banner, Advertising, &c.	$ 99.15
Knapsacks, 100 "Shorts."	252.50
Lettering Knapsacks.	10.00
Company's Proportion of Band Expenses at Readville	100.00
Carried forward,	$461.65

Brought forward,	$461,65
Stove, Tinware, Bread, Milk, Provisions and Sundries at Readville	320.21
Band Fund, Drummers' Trimmings and Gloves	33.55
Thanksgiving, Expenses at New Berne	53.86
Company's Proportion of Expense of Colors for Fifth Rhode Island Regiment	20.00
	$889.27

SUNDRY EXPENSES AS FOLLOWS:

Load wood 75c., Q. M. Bush $1.87, Sutler $2.23	$4.85
Stove, J. Lewis $18.00 ; Sutler Hunt's Bill $31.80	49.80
Q. M. Bush, extra rations, $7.00, Lantern $2.00	9.00
Hinges for Ventilator $1.00, Use of Oven $1.50	2.50
Paper and Printing $3.30, Stove Polish 30c., Leather $1.00.	4.60
Nails, Brush, Comb and Glass $1.85, Onions $2.50	4.35
Water-pails 75c., Planes $3.00, Tin-box Covers $3.00	6.75
Fish $2.00, Potatoes $4 05, Tobacco $3.00, Broom 50c	9.55
Oil 15c., Blacking and Brush $1.00, use of room $2.00	3.15
Cleaning Rooms $3.75, bill Q. M. Bush $14.70	18 45
Repairing Stove $5.00, Sundries at Little Washington $2 30	7.30
Condensed Milk	53.25
Sugar $10.64, Coffee $8.50, Fish and Potatoes $3.40	22.54
Dried Apples $3.60, Tripe $4.20, Q. M. Bush$1.00	8.60
Hinges, Lock and Paper $2 15, Emery Cloth $7.50	9.65
Blacking 90c., Coffee 90c., Cleaning and Whitewashing $6.75	17.65
Expenses Entertainment "D" and "E"	14.75
Herrings, Pickles, &c	9.75
Blacking, Brushes and Paper	3.00
5 dozen Letters E	5.00
Cleaning Quarters	2 25
Lemons $5.00, Cutting Hair $5.50, Cheese $6.18	16 68
Donation to Colored Boatman Washington	9.00

SUNDRY BILLS FOR SUPPLIES.

Dibble & Co	$160.62	
C. Hunt & Co	245 60	
J. Lewis & Co	18.00	
J. B. Steele & Co	45.80	
Lovejoy & Co	6.50	
H. D. Hawley & Co., Gloves	47.05	
		523.57
Company Supper at Parker's		164.12
Opening Armory Boylston Street and Advertising Pay		6 87
On account Expenses T. L. Barnes		150.00
		1,136.98
U. S. Shortage on Clothing, &c		19.77
Company E Associates Fund		23.65
		$2,069.67

THE MONUMENT.

About the first of August, 1877, the writer (representing Company E in the 44th Regimental Association), received a notification of a meeting of the Executive Committee, to be held at Col. Lee's office, Boston. At that meeting, eight companies being represented, it was voted to call a meeting of the Regimental Association, on Friday, August 17th, at 81 Franklin Street, to take into consideration the question of parading on the 17th of September, at the dedication of the Soldiers' and Sailors' Monument, erected by the City of Boston in memory of those who laid down their lives in the slaveholders' rebellion. At the meeting of the Regimental Association it was unanimously voted to parade on the 17th of September.

" E " did well at this parade, turning out twenty-one men. We formed at the head-quarters, 81 Franklin Street, about nine o'clock in the forenoon, in two platoons, single rank, the first platoon under command of Capt. Richardson in his old uniform. The second under Sergt. J. Fred Moore. The following men were on hand: Capt. S. W. Richardson, Acting First Lieut. J. F. Moore, G. H. Adams, W. R. Adams, Bowman, Clough, Currier, Derby, Dyer, Flagg, Magoun, Millar, Pettingill, H. T. Pierce, Pulsifer, Ramsay, Russell, Tower, Trott, Whall, Wyeth. From the head-quarters we marched to the Tremont Street Bridge, waiting an hour or so for the column to form, taking our place at last, and marching to the music of our old drum corps, who had kindly volunteered for the occasion, and had been practicing the old tunes for a week. The march was about eight miles long ; up Shawmut Avenue, as far as Roxbury, down Washington Street to Summer, then across to State Street, where we had the pleasure of marching once more ; then by the City Hall and State House—at the latter place marching in review by the Governor ; thence to Charles Street, *past* the Common where the dedicatory services *to which we had been invited, had, to all appearances been held.* Here Lieut.-Col. Cabot dismissed the 44th, probably for the last time, and " E," with the drum corps, *took the first horse car* for the " Commonwealth," where we arrived about 5 P.M., dusty and tired of course ; but well pleased with ourselves and with the manner in which our friends had received us on the route. After a short rest, we betook ourselves to the dining-room, where a nice dinner awaited us, which we found no difficulty in mastering ; breaking up about seven o'clock.

––––

And now, comrades of " E," although I know it is proper, for one who writes a book, to say all he intends to, of a direct personal nature, in the preface, I cannot put the final period to these " Leaves " without adding a word or two.

Of course, each man had his own experiences, as well as ideas, perhaps totally different from mine, but as I received impressions then, I have embodied them now in this. Our short experience in the army, I think, did most of us good. Physically a few were injured, and in consequence have passed to their long home. Their stay with us will ever be fresh in our memory.

The restraint we were under, and the discipline we received, though often irksome, taught us a lesson, which perhaps, we could not have learned otherwise, and will remain with us all our lives.

We have forgotten the hard part, the rough edges have worn smooth, and we look ahead with much pleasure, each succeeding year, to our re-unions, where officers and men meet, and talk over old times, when we were " Boys of E."

No. " 34."